The moment of truth...

"We, the elders of the Bluefin Clan, have made our selection," Dyonis announced, and everyone grew quiet. Nia could barely believe this was happening—she was so close to seeing her dream become real. *She* would soon be one of the honored few charged with keeping Atlantis safe and beautiful. She would learn the secrets of the past from the Farworlders and help keep the future peaceful.

"And we believe this young person represents our best hope for the future of Atlantis," Dyonis continued. "I now call upon that one to come forward and accept the honor and challenge that our selection bestows. I call upon . . . Garun!"

Nia's jaw dropped. She watched openmouthed as Garun sprang from the rungs and swam awkwardly to tread water beside Dyonis. As she heard the cheering around her, Nia felt dizzy, her head spinning slightly as if she were ill. *No, no, it isn't possible! How could they have chosen Garun over me? How?*

Enjoy all three books in the *Water* Trilogy:

Water

BOOK ONE

ASCENSION

KARA DALKEY

AVON BOOKS

An Imprint of HarperCollinsPublishers

For information address
HarperCollins Children's Books, a division of
HarperCollins Publishers, 1350 Avenue of the Americas,
New York, NY 10019.

 Produced by 17th Street Productions,
an Alloy, Inc. company
151 West 26th Street, New York, NY 10001

Library of Congress Catalog Card Number: 2001118041
ISBN 0-06-440808-6

First Avon edition, 2002

AVON TRADEMARK REG. U.S. PAT. OFF.
AND IN OTHER COUNTRIES,
MARCA REGISTRADA, HECHO EN U.S.A.

Visit us on the World Wide Web!
www.harperteen.com

Chapter One

"Nia! Watch out!"

But Niniane of the Bluefin Clan, known as Nia to all, arrowed her body, easily swimming through the narrow space between the marble columns of the building beside her. She emerged on the other side without even a scratch. "Watch out for what?" she asked with a wide-eyed, innocent grin as she swam back to her friend Callimar's side.

Callimar narrowed her golden eyes behind a fringe of deep-green hair. "Watch out that you don't show off so much that you become an annoyance to your friends." She gave Nia a playful slap with her tail.

"Was I showing off?" Nia asked, although she knew very well that she was. "I thought I was practicing. Training. For the Trials." Nia did a back somersault, the fins along the backs of her arms and legs guiding her smoothly through the water. Her long, silvery hair flowed in an elegant arc behind her. She took pride in the strength and grace of her body and knew that if she were chosen for the Ascension, her physical abilities would be part of the reason.

The City of Atlantis seemed to sparkle more than ever this day. The high-towered palaces of the noble clans, carved from coral stone, marble, and malachite, some faced with shimmering mother-of-pearl, glimmered all around them. The blue-green bioluminescent light from the enormous globe lamps that hung over the city seemed to glow brighter. The lamps provided the primary light to this dim world in the depths of the sea. To the mermyds, sunlight was a thing mentioned only in fairy tales and history books.

Nia wondered whether the sea siphons and filtration tunnels were working harder than usual today—the water seemed so fresh and bubbly and full of energy-giving oxygen. Or perhaps she was merely giddy, knowing she was the perfect age at the perfect time in the perfect place. She was sixteen, a prime age for a new Avatar. The Low and High Councils that together ruled Atlantis were made up of ten Avatars, chosen from the mermyd population, and ten Farworlder kings. Each mermyd Avatar would join with a Farworlder to form a pair, since the powerful Farworlder kings could express their thoughts only through a special connection with a mermyd Avatar. And now one of the ten Avatars and his Farworlder king had just reached the age for retirement, meaning that a new Avatar would be chosen for the Low Council, along with a new Farworlder king for the High Council. Nia had every reason to believe that she could be the one participating in the upcoming Ascension —being joined with a Farworlder king and taking her place among the ten Avatars of the Low Council. She had all the important qualifications, and everyone in her family—probably everyone in her entire *clan*—knew how much she dreamed of taking on the responsibility. From the day she could speak, she'd begged her grandfather, an Avatar himself, to tell her stories of his experiences. The idea of finally being able to learn the deepest secrets known only to Farworlders and their Avatars held infinite appeal to Nia.

"Not to burst your bubble," Callimar said, interrupting Nia's thoughts, "but the last I recall hearing of them, the Trials did not involve threading yourself through obstacles like sea spider cord through a fish bone needle. Or doing gymnastics."

"How do you know?" Nia asked, doing a forward somersault this time, keeping her legs straight and perfectly together. "Maybe they'll change things this time."

"And maybe fish will grow legs like you have," said Callimar. Some mermyds had fishlike fins for their lower bodies and some had two legs like Nia's, and either sort could be born into a mermyd family. Only the Farworlders knew why. "Really, Nia, I think you should have been born into the Dolphin Clan, not the Bluefins."

Callimar was one of the few mermyds Nia knew who were so sensitive about birthclan. Callimar was of the Sunfish Clan, a noble family whose members often held important positions in Atlantean government. Nia's clan, the Bluefin, was not quite so illustrious, but Nia was proud of her family nonetheless. "Callimar, you're beginning to sound like my mother."

"I'm beginning to age, just watching you," Callimar countered. "But I suppose you have all that nervous energy to use up."

"Nervous? Me? I don't think so!" Nia replied. "I'm perfectly calm."

Callimar laughed. "You don't fool me," she teased. "The water is several degrees warmer near you, and this time it's not because you're thinking of a certain Stingray."

Nia blushed but turned her face away to hide it. She did not want to be tricked into talking about Cephan right now. "You're just jealous," Nia argued, "that you aren't being considered to represent your clan in the Trials."

Each clan would choose a member to compete for the

role of Avatar, and from what Nia could guess, she would be the obvious choice for the Bluefins.

"Me? Hah! I would have been terrified to be chosen," Callimar said. She paused, frowning. "No, actually I would have been terrified of *winning* the Trials and becoming an Avatar," she added, tossing her head slightly. "To undergo the ritual of the Naming and be nearly poisoned to death? To share my deepest thoughts all the rest of my days with a creature that looks like a big squid and thinks like . . . I don't know what? That's enough to scare any sane mermyd. I'm glad it looks like my brother will be the one competing for the Sunfish Clan, not me."

"Now you're the one being silly," Nia said. "Nearly every Avatar-to-be has survived the Naming. And the sharing of minds with such peaceful and wise creatures as the Farworlders is supposed to be incredible." It certainly seemed to Nia that it would be incredible—*beyond* incredible, in fact.

"So they say," Callimar murmured. "But I would bet there's a great deal the Avatars don't tell us about what the experience is truly like."

"There is a lot they don't tell," Nia agreed. She swished her silvery hair thoughtfully. "I wonder if Farworlders can truly see into the future, or if a joined king and Avatar can truly move mountains with their thoughts alone."

"I suppose, if you win the Trials, you'll find out," Callimar said.

"Yes, I suppose so." The thought gave Nia more than a small thrill.

"I had thought," Callimar said carefully, "that you were nervous because so many people would be staring at you, watching you."

Nia sighed, blowing bubbles between her lips. Callimar knew that Nia sometimes worried about the way she so closely resembled a land-dweller, one of the mouth-breathers, as humankind was called. As a young mermyd, she had been teased about her small nose, small eyes, and delicate neck gills. Even past childhood, her skin had remained smooth, growing hardly any scales to speak of. And Nia had almost no webbing between her fingers and toes. The fact that she was a two-legged mermyd instead of a fish-tailed mermyd only made the resemblance stronger. Nia cast a glance at Callimar, noting once again the way Callimar's large golden eyes, fin-shaped ears, and emerald-green hair made her the perfect picture of mermyd beauty.

"I expect," Nia said, "that if I am chosen to compete, I'll be too busy and excited to even think about that." Nia paused to drift a moment. She gazed up at the crystal dome high above them that arched over the entire city, keeping the crushing pressure of the sea above them at bay. The Dome was Atlantis's protection, and its prison, thanks to the warlike land-dwellers. Over a thousand years had passed, and still the ancient prejudice remained. The greed and brutality of the mouthbreathers was legendary—they were spoken of as threatening monsters to frighten misbehaving mermyd children. Any mermyd who happened to look like a mouthbreather could expect some teasing in life.

"Of course you will," Callimar said. "I'm sorry. I shouldn't even have brought that up."

The two of them swam on together in silence, through the canyonlike streets between the tall palaces. Many other mermyds around them were hurrying home, for over half the families in Atlantis would be choosing their young candidate for the Trials this evening.

To keep her worries from growing, Nia reminded herself of the reasons why she should be chosen to represent the Bluefins. One, the first two Trials were tests of strength and speed and Nia would excel at those. Two, she was good at solving puzzles and mazes, which would help with Trials three and four. As to her magical ability, well, no one ever said she didn't have enough, only that her skills were . . . different. Unusual. Hard to measure. *That might even be an advantage too*, Nia thought.

At last, Nia and Callimar came to the palace of the Bluefin Clan. Nia gazed up at the tower of coral stone, with its mosaic of turquoise-and-pink shell. The entrance to the Grand Meeting Hall was up on the fifth floor. Golden light beamed out from the entryway, and she thought she heard music. She felt her neck gills ripple and swell, trying to pull more calming oxygen from the water. She tugged at her pale-green chemise of sea-silk, fearing there might be too little fabric in the wrong places. "Do you think I'm dressed well enough?"

"Will you stop worrying?" Callimar sighed. "They're your family and clan. They have to take you in. Remember that. Now I must leave you to go on by yourself, or else those handsome Orca guardsmen at the entrance will have to wrestle me away. Hmm. Perhaps I'll go in with you after all."

"What, and get me into trouble with both your clan and mine? Go on, or I'll just stop here." The choosing of a contestant for the Trials was a very private affair for each clan. No outsiders were permitted, not even to observe.

"All right," Callimar agreed. "Well, good luck, Nia. Although I doubt you'll need any." Callimar smiled and gave Nia a brief hug about the shoulders, then turned and swam away.

Nia gazed up one more time at the great crystal dome. She knew that once upon a time, long ago, mermyds had traveled wherever they pleased in the great oceans of Earth. Now only a few trusted scouts and hunters were permitted to swim beyond the Dome, and whatever they found beyond they revealed only to the High and Low Councils. Nia wondered if there were even any land-dwellers left. Given their warlike reputation, surely such creatures were bound to wipe one another out one day. *I hope,* she thought, *that if I become an Avatar, I'll know more of these things.*

She turned and swam up, up, up to the fifth story of the Bluefin Palace. The black-haired Orca guardsmen looked very elegant and official in their black-and-white uniforms. Nia nodded at them, regally she hoped, as they looked her over. "Hey, Round-ears," said the one on the left with a flirtatious smile, "glad you could make it— they've been asking if we'd seen you yet."

Nia tried to glare at him, blushing furiously. The guardsman appeared to have only meant to tease her gently, but the teasing still stung. "My grandfather would not be pleased to hear you address me thus," she said in her most mock-formal tone.

"Ah. Your pardon, Lady Niniane," the Orca said with a slight bow. His cheeks grew faintly blue, and Nia realized he was embarrassed.

She sighed, not knowing whether to be flattered or annoyed. She hadn't even wanted to mention her illustrious grandfather, as if his name were a magical phrase to make all underlings cower. Callimar would have said she had every right to do so, but Callimar had gone home.

Nia smiled and swam past the guardsmen nonchalantly. The Grand Meeting Hall of the Bluefin was festively decorated with puffer-fish lanterns and garlands of kelp, and the members of the clan were brightly dressed. Nia was an only child, but she had many cousins, at whom she nodded and smiled and said hello. Her cousins had often defended her in childhood against the few would-be bullies of other houses. As the saying went, "Family defends family and clan defends clan, just as dolphins against the sharks band."

Nia heard a familiar booming voice from one corner of the Grand Hall. It was her grandfather, Dyonis, holding forth on politics with her parents. Dyonis was a hale, elderly mermyd with a long, flowing white beard and white hair and lively sea-green eyes. But he hadn't been given the nickname Whale-lungs for nothing.

"I assure you, duties that are purely ceremonial are always the best kind!" he was saying jovially.

"But don't you ever miss being on the Council, Dyonis?" Nia's mother, Tyra, asked him as Nia approached. "Surely it must be difficult to watch the decision-making from the sidelines."

"Oh, hardly," Dyonis said with a wave of his hand. "You must understand, it's very peaceful, being retired. I was just telling Thaumas yesterday how much he and his king will enjoy it. I, myself, was quite pleased to be replaced with younger, healthier stock, and now Ar'an and I can play endless games of mahresso. . . . Ah, Nia! There you are!"

Nia brightened as her grandfather noticed her. Dyonis had never belittled her or treated her like a child, and Nia loved him for that. She wondered if there were clues to be gained from his welcoming her so warmly, that perhaps she was indeed to be the chosen one. The decision had been largely his, which was another reason Nia knew her chances were good. Dyonis had always adored her. And he certainly knew how badly she wanted to be an Avatar.

"Yes, here I am," she said, not knowing what more to say.

"Ah. Niniane." Her father, Pontus, gave her no more than a curt nod of acknowledgment. He was a portly mermyd, and Nia couldn't help but think that his head resembled the puffer-fish lanterns adorning the walls.

"There you are!" Tyra said. With a slight frown, she tugged at the straps of Nia's dress. "What was the matter with the pale-blue shift that I said you should wear to tonight's gathering? It is closer to the clan color, after all."

"Um, a baby squid down at the market spit some ink on it. Don't worry, Mother, it wasn't much, and I'll get it clean." Actually, the blue shift was too loose and voluminous, and Nia thought it made her look like a blobby jellyfish. "Callimar told me this dress would be fine." Nia knew that her mother wouldn't dare contradict the opinion of a Sunfish. "And, besides, she said it isn't really the thing anymore to wear the clan colors at every party— just for the big events."

"This isn't a big event?" her mother asked with raised brows. "My, you are confident tonight, aren't you?" She paused, exhaling deeply. "Well, I suppose Callimar must know fashion, mustn't she? We Bluefins should listen up." Tyra winked in self-mockery. Nia's mother was very proud of having married into the Bluefin Clan, having been born a Seabass, but even Tyra thought the Sunfish acted a bit too high-and-mighty now and then.

Upon marriage, a mermyd couple could choose which

clan to formally affiliate themselves with, and usually the clan of higher social rank was chosen. Tyra made it quite clear that she expected Nia to marry up as well, perhaps even to one of the snobbish Sunfish. Never mind that there wasn't a single Sunfish that Nia could stand, besides Callimar.

No, Nia was quite content with her secret crush, Cephan, even if he was a Stingray—someone very different from her own clan.

Nia couldn't help thinking how being chosen for Ascension as the next Avatar would even solve that problem. Avatars could choose to marry anyone they wished, or not at all, and no one could say anything against it— not even meddling mothers.

"Go find yourself a comfortable spot on the lattice, Nia!" Dyonis chimed in, greeting her with a broad smile. "I will make the announcement soon; I do not wish to keep my kin waiting. And, frankly, I always hated giving speeches. I would just as soon have this done."

Nia somehow doubted that, given how her grandfather seemed to love to be the center of attention at every gathering. But she smiled and swam to where the lattice had been hung. It was a tall, cylindrical structure of soft sea-weed rope and was the best way ever found to have a group of mermyd gathered close together in assembly. Nia had read that land-dwellers would gather together seated on chairs or on benches. There were still some preserved in the Atlantean Museum. To Nia they seemed like such silly contraptions, almost useless underwater, because what would keep you from floating away?

Besides, staying absolutely still for long periods could be dangerous to mermyds—their gills could not extract enough oxygen without water moving past. Either the water must move or the mermyd must, or else the mermyd would drift into sleep, and then unconsciousness, and then suffocating death.

In a rope lattice, on the other hand, mermyds could lay their arms across the rope in front, hang their legs or tail over the rope behind, swing and sway gently, or wriggle in place. With many mermyds arrayed side by side, and one over the other, ten lattice rungs high, the water in the chamber was kept flowing by all their movement.

Best of all, the Bluefin Palace had the privilege of being near the rim of the city, closer to the great filtration tubes whose suction kept the water of Atlantis clean and kept currents flowing. The water was cleaner here and felt fresher to the gills. Nearest the rim, right next to the Dome, was where the current was fastest, and Nia, as a child, would sometimes ride the rim current, once letting it take her all the way around the city. Her mother had had fits when she found out.

Nia found a rung high enough to give her a good view of the center platform where Dyonis would speak, but low enough that she could swim down quickly if—*when*—she was called as the chosen candidate. There were few other mermyds on that row, so Nia could stretch out for a while in peace and try to recollect what she had planned to say in her acceptance speech.

Suddenly, her ropes bounced and jostled as someone swam into the lattice beside her.

"Greetings, cousin," came a familiar nasal tone.

Nia's mood dimmed considerably. It was Garun.

Nia wished she could have even slightly more respect for her cousin. He was near her age, seventeen. And he had two legs and somewhat humanlike features, like her. But he was about as dull and uninteresting as a mermyd could be. Even his hair, skin, and eyes were a pale blue-gray. He was studious, not very athletic, and completely unambitious. He was an archivist at the Farworlder Palace, and he was destined to be an archivist forever. Nia couldn't imagine a more boring job, or a more boring mermyd to be in it. Except for his occasional tendency to make a point of seeming smarter than everyone else, Garun was hardly noticeable at all.

"Good evening, Garun," Nia said, hoping he wouldn't stay beside her. She wanted to share her moment of victory with someone more interesting. "Were you thinking this was the best spot for a good view?" she asked him, trying to keep the irritation out of her voice. "Actually, someone told me that you can hear better from about two rungs up."

Garun blinked at her as if she had just told him that she liked to eat green worms. "This *is* the rung for the eligible candidates. Didn't you *know*? Isn't it obvious that I would be here?"

"I—I . . . of course," Nia stammered. "I was just joking." *Does Garun think he's an eligible candidate? Surely no one seriously intended to nominate him. Perhaps his parents bought him a place on the roster to boost his pride.* Not that Garun's huge ego needed that.

But Nia knew exactly who her real competition was— her cousin Ichthus. He was another good athlete like her, maybe even better—but about as bright as a lantern fish. Then there was Bathys. She was only fifteen, and although she was bright, she wasn't at all magically gifted. Sure enough, Nia saw the two of them heading toward the rung where she and Garun were, but she didn't feel intimidated. In fact the sight of them only boosted her own confidence.

Garun sighed, blowing bubbles out of his pursed, pale lips. "Dyonis is going to turn *this* way when he makes his final announcement. Our elders will be arrayed on *those* rungs," he said, nodding at the lattice on the other side of the cylinder, "so they can see us when the name is announced. That name is going to be mine."

It was Nia's turn to blink. "Yours?" She wondered if he was joking, or if he really was that deluded.

I suppose spending all your days in the Archives might make you out of touch with the rest of the world, she thought. *But didn't anyone try to discourage him? Yes, he has mental gifts, but the first two Trials are physical tests of speed and strength.* Garun couldn't even finish one of those races, much less win.

"Well. Good luck," she said halfheartedly.

"I won't need luck," Garun boasted in his usual way.

Nia sighed and decided not to be rude. *Let him have his hopes while he can*, she told herself, letting the excitement wash over her again as she imagined what she'd feel when she heard her name announced.

Bathys eagerly swam over and took the rung beside Nia. She looked so very young, with her wide, eager golden eyes and bouncy yellow-green hair. In fact, all of her was bouncy—Bathys could hardly keep her tail and hands from flapping all over. "Isn't this exciting?" she kept asking.

"Yes, yes, it is," Nia said with a sisterly smile. *At least I won't have to worry about still water in this rung. Bathys will keep it moving just fine all by herself.*

Ichthus took the rung just on the other side of Garun. Ichthus didn't talk much, but you could tell from the light in his eyes and his great big grin that he was just as excited as Bathys.

The lattice began to fill up with other mermyds. As Garun had said, her parents and other elders of the Bluefin Clan took rungs on the other side, in a good position to watch the competitors.

At last, Dyonis swam into the center of the cylinder, above the platform on the floor, and raised his arms. "Good evening, those of the Bluefin Clan! On this night, we choose one of our kind to be the symbol of our honor, our strength, and our wisdom in the upcoming Trials. The Trials that will elevate the one who will be the new Avatar into the Low Council.

"As always, we choose one of our young, someone whose mind is still growing, and whose growth therefore can be guided through the watchful care of a Farworlder, eventually achieving greater wisdom than any mermyd alone can know. Someone whose body is strong, so that it may withstand the Naming, and will have many years of healthful life ahead to share with a king. . . ."

Well, that takes Bathys and Garun off the list, Nia thought, biting back a smile. She could barely believe this was happening—she was so close to seeing her dream become real. *She* would soon be one of the honored few charged with keeping Atlantis safe and beautiful. She would learn the secrets of the past from the Farworlders and help keep the future peaceful and . . .

". . . Someone who has new thoughts as to how things might be done, and who is not weighed down by years of tradition and habit. Someone with a talent for concentrat ing his or her mind, which is essential for the practice of magic, so that the new Avatar can assist in keeping Atlantis running well and safe from harm."

And that is where my parents say I am weakest, Nia thought, shifting. *They say I am easily distracted. I can't believe Dyonis said he hates giving speeches. He's talked so long. Who is he going to pick? I can hardly stand it!* She gripped the rope in front of her so hard her palms hurt.

"We choose our best," Dyonis went on, "in hopes that

the Councils, High and Low, will look upon our candidate's efforts in the Trials and deem him or her worthy of being one of their number.

"We, the elders of the Bluefin Clan, have made our selection, and we believe this young person represents our best hope for the future of Atlantis. I now call upon that one to come forward and accept the honor and challenge that our selection bestows. I call upon . . . Garun!"

Nia's jaw dropped. She watched openmouthed as Garun sprang from the rungs and swam awkwardly to tread water beside Dyonis. As she heard the cheering around her, Nia felt dizzy, her head spinning slightly as if she were ill. *No, no, it isn't possible! How could they have chosen Garun over me? How?*

Chapter Two

Nia swam back and forth through the malachite arch-ways, unable to remain still for even a short time. She was currently on duty as a palace guard in the Farworlder Royal Nursery. It was her job, for several hours every other day, to watch over the offspring of the Farworlder kings. Although it was a well-respected post, Nia had been anxious to leave it behind when she assumed her responsibilities as Avatar. Watching over Farworlders was one thing—but watching over the entire city of Atlantis was her true dream.

Nia sighed, staring at the bubbles that formed in the water in front of her. She hadn't stayed at the Bluefin gathering the night before, after Garun's name was announced. It had been rude of her, she knew, but she just couldn't manage to congratulate him. *It's not just because I lost,* she thought, *but because the pride of the Bluefin Clan is at stake. Won't we make fools of ourselves with Garun representing us?*

She had been unable to hide her disappointment. She had not dared to speak to Dyonis, fearing what she might say, but Nia had glanced at him before she went out the door. He had gazed back at her with sorrow and regret, so he clearly knew how shocked and devastated the announcement had left her. Then why had he made such a surprising choice?

Nia moved her gaze to the little baby Farworlders, snug in their translucent, opalescent shells. They waved their little shrimp-pink tentacles at her, as if sensing her pain.

Back and forth she swam past the rows of squidlings, as she considered them. Of course that wasn't what the Farworlders truly were—they were an alien race of creatures who had come to Atlantis eons ago when the ship they were traveling on landed there. But as babies, they resembled small squids, which was why she referred to them as such. Nia checked to see that each infant had a little bag full of plankton and shredded seaweed to eat. She also made sure there were no spots on the babies' transparent skins that might indicate infection. There wasn't much else for her to do, other than look officious and protective if someone came by. The little Farworlders pretty much looked after themselves.

Even if the job wasn't always exciting, Nia enjoyed

being with the infant Farworlders. In fact, she often suspected one of them was trying to communicate, magically, with her. Sometimes, when she swam quietly on duty, she could almost feel the little one probing at her mind, reaching out with tentacles of thought, trying to sense her. Making her see or hear things. *Practicing*, she thought, *for when it will be joined to an Avatar.*

This was something Nia had quickly learned she couldn't tell other mermyds. Her friends told her she was making things up—no Farworlder could share thoughts with a mermyd it wasn't joined to. Only during the Naming, by receiving in one's blood the secretions of the Farworlder's oculus, could a mermyd even begin to have such an ability. The Farworlders' oculus glands were the sources of their magic, and it was only because of these glands that they could establish the strong mental connections with mermyd Avatars. The glands also allowed Farworlders to sense things about the Unis—the fabric of space and time—and perceive images in the unfolding of fate. There were limitations to these abilities, but the idea of actually being able to *sense* the future had been one of the reasons Nia had longed to be an Avatar. She was always looking forward to the future, anxious to plan and develop exciting new things for Atlantis. Being an Avatar would have meant being linked to a Farworlder with whom she could have shared all these dreams.

But you are not an Avatar, and you aren't going to be, Nia reminded herself. Which was why she had to keep quiet about the mental connection she was sure she felt with the infant Farworlder. She didn't want everyone around her to think she was crazy.

Nia felt strands of her hair being tugged. She turned . . . but no one was there. She felt a tickle on her left arm and scratched. Then she heard a chittering from one of the baby Farworlders behind her, playing tricks on her again. She sighed. "Please, little one, I'm not in the mood to play today."

She felt a touch on her cheek, as if someone was trying to comfort her. Nia knew which little Farworlder it had come from—the one that had become her favorite, third from the left, first row. It was a bit larger than the others and more playful, always wiggling its tentacles at her whenever she swam by. Nia had even begun playing back, letting it wrap its tentacles around her fingers. But Nia had always been careful to avoid the tentacle with the circle of tiny talons on the tip. Those talons would be used by the Farworlder during a Naming to mark an Avatar, to inject the secretion to complete the joining of minds.

Nia swam over to it and bent to smile at the little one in

the shell. "You again. What are you up to this time? Do you want to get me in trouble by making people think I'm crazy? Just you wait—someday you might become a king, and then you'll join your mind to a mermyd and know how we suffer for your sake."

Then all the little Farworlders began chittering, clacking their tiny beaks. "Oh, what *is* it?" Nia cried, exasperated. She felt another tickle, this time on her right shoulder blade, and she spun around.

"Now you stop—" she started, breaking off when she saw that someone was actually there.

"Cephan!" she blurted out, her eyes widening as she saw his face. She hoped she wasn't blushing blue, as she usually did when he was around.

"Stop what?" he asked.

"Um . . ." Her gills fluttered, making it hard to speak. "You know, you can't be an effective guardian if you let just anyone sneak up behind you."

"I . . . I was distracted."

She was even more distracted now. Distracted by Cephan's thick, curly hair that was such a dark green it was almost black. Distracted by his deep, deep blue eyes. She felt the blush rise to her cheeks as she continued to stare. Cephan had a powerful fishtail with glossy scales the color of his hair. He was nearly perfect, in her opinion. They'd been flirting for a while now, and she hoped his coming here meant he felt the same way about her that she did about him.

"You know you shouldn't be here," she finally said.

Cephan grinned. "And that's why I'm here," he said, his eyes gleaming. "Well, and also to see you." Then he turned to address the squidlings. "Hey, little fellows! Look what I've brought you!" He pulled from a pouch at his waist a tiny green sphere of some transparent material. There was an air bubble at the center of it. Cephan let go of the sphere right over one of the Farworlders' shells, and the thing slowly dropped through the water. The baby Farworlder reached up with its tentacles and batted the sphere away. This sent the sphere over toward another squidling, who reached up and tossed it to yet another. Pretty soon the sphere was slowly bouncing between the shells, and the baby Farworlders were chittering merrily.

"I don't understand," Cephan said. "We mermyds, as children, get toys all the time, but these creatures are never given any toys."

"They're very delicate," Nia explained, "and they can be easily bruised or have tentacles torn off. And . . . what *is* that thing, anyway?"

Cephan leaned toward her conspiratorially. "It's from the land-dwellers. Shh. Don't tell anyone."

"Land-dwellers?" Nia cried in amazement. "How did you get a thing made by land-dwellers?"

"I have a cousin who's a hunter. He went out into the Greater Ocean for a while. He brought that back with him, among other things."

"You know someone who went Outside? What did he see? Are there any land-dwellers left? What did he tell you?"

Cephan laughed. "I guess you're pretty interested in the world out there," he said, raising his brows. "Well. I can't tell you much, as my cousin was sworn to secrecy. But I can say this: There are plenty of land-dwellers, all over the world. But their ships aren't as big as they used to be, before the Sinking. Anyway, *that* object is a float some land-dwellers tie to their fishing nets."

"Ahh." Nia admired the rare object for a moment and then started to worry that she'd get in trouble if it were found in the nursery. She snatched it while it was in midbounce and held it tightly in her hand. "I'd better keep it for now."

"You're spoiling their fun," he complained.

"They aren't supposed to have fun. One of them is soon going to be picked to be the king for whoever wins the Trials, and I want them all to stay healthy."

"Ah. The Trials. I heard about Garun being chosen as the Bluefins' competitor," Cephan said gently. "I am so sorry, Nia. I know how much you wanted to compete."

"I must accept the elders' decision," Nia admitted. "But I don't understand it. Garun is . . . a nobody! A nothing!"

Cephan cocked his head to the side. "Even those who seem to be nobodies and nothings may hide amazing talents, Nia."

"Not Garun," she retorted. "Yes, he *is* very smart, and I've heard he has magical strengths. But I can't imagine he will do well." She played with the toy in her palm, running her fingers over it. "You don't think it was me, do you?" she asked softly. "Did I do something wrong that made them choose someone else?"

"Impossible," Cephan said. He moved closer to her, and her heart began to beat more quickly. "I can't think of any reason why they didn't choose you," he said sincerely, meeting her gaze. "It was probably just politics. And don't ask me to explain politics. As we say in the Lower Depths, 'Bottom-feeders can only see the underbellies of those who swim above.'"

"You are *not* a bottom-feeder," Nia said, staring up into his eyes. "You are more kind and noble in spirit than half the Sunfish mermyds I've met."

Cephan blushed a little and looked down. "If kindness were a qualification, they should have chosen *you* over all the other Bluefins," he said. "And you are certainly stronger and faster than Garun. And, besides, the little Farworlders like you."

Now it was Nia's turn to smile and blush. "Thanks, but I don't think being able to entertain the Royal Nursery is a suitable qualification for Avatar. Or else you'd be chosen just for giving them a toy."

"Why not? This is a very important job, what you do," Cephan argued. "Don't think it isn't, just because it isn't more public. The High Council wouldn't have appointed you to this post if they didn't think you were trustworthy. What could be more precious than their offspring? Besides, think how much you'd have to entertain one Farworlder if you're joined to it all your life. What could be more important for an Avatar than the skill of getting along with Farworlders?"

Nia bit her lip. "Apparently it's not as important as being . . . whatever Garun is," she muttered.

Cephan shook his head. "We have another saying Down Below: 'The ways of the elders are as twisted as a narwhal's tusk.' I think they've made a big mistake. However, the Bluefins' loss may be my gain." He paused, and his eyes took on a strange glint. "I *was* chosen to compete for the Stingray Clan," he said.

"You were? Why didn't you tell me sooner? Oh, Cephan, congratulations!" Nia hugged him around the neck without even stopping to think.

"Easy there!" Cephan said, as he was nearly pushed back against a Farworlder crèche. Nia moved back, blushing like crazy at what she'd just done. Then, as the hair on Cephan's forehead floated upward, Nia noticed a long, red scar along his hairline.

"Cephan, what happened?" Nia reached up, but Cephan gently guided her hand away.

"It's nothing," he said. "I hit my head against the edge of a filtration tube. I just wasn't watching where I was going. It still stings a little. But my physician says it will be fine in time for the competition."

"Oh, that's good," Nia said, relieved. Then a new thought struck her. "I don't know what I'll do during the trials. My family loyalty should make me want Garun to win, but I can't help being happy that you have a better chance of winning."

Cephan's smile faded slightly. "I don't know if you're right about that," he said. "Garun still must have a better chance, considering that your clan has a former Avatar as its elder."

"The Councils aren't supposed to be biased," Nia said. "Even if mermyds can be, when a mermyd joins with a Farworlder it's supposed to make them both wise."

"So they say. But who knows how much one mind dominates the other? Only the Avatars can speak. Perhaps it has all been a giant hoax, and it's really just the mermyds who rule."

"Cephan! That's disrespectful," Nia teased. "I'm surprised your clan chose you when you swim around talking like that."

Cephan lifted his head proudly. "They had very good reason to choose me," he said.

"I'm sure they did," Nia said. A frown tugged at her lips as she thought about how much she still didn't know about Cephan's life when they weren't together. "Um . . . like what?" she asked.

Cephan bit his lip. "I can't say," he blurted out.

Nia's eyes widened. "But Cephan, you *have* to tell me now," she begged.

Cephan looked at her, obviously torn. Then he glanced around them, even though no one was there aside from the infant Farworlders. "You remember I said that nobodies and nothings can hide amazing secrets?" he asked, a note of excitement entering his voice.

"You aren't a *nobody*, Cephan," she chided him. "At least, not to me," she added, wondering if she was being too forward. "So, what's your secret?" she pressed.

"I have a second job besides tending the filtration tubes."

Nia waited, but he didn't go on. "That's it? Many mermyds do more than one thing," she said.

Cephan sighed and rolled his eyes. "It's a very significant job, the only one of its kind in Atlantis. It's a job that proves me highly responsible and capable and trustworthy."

"So . . . what is it?" she prodded.

"I can't tell you."

Nia burst out laughing and covered her mouth to keep from spitting bubbles at him. "Can't tell me? This is more elaborate than your usual jokes, Cephan."

Cephan leaned close. "It's not a joke. I can't tell you. But maybe . . . maybe I can show you."

"Oh?"

He paused. "I really shouldn't, you know. But it's so important to me that you know everything about me. And I know I can trust you." He seemed to be talking more to himself than to her now. "But you have to be willing to do a very brave thing," he said finally. "It could be dangerous."

"Dangerous?" Nia asked, raising her brows in disbelief.

"You'll have to come with me to the Lower Depths."

"Oh. I see." Most noble mermyds didn't venture below the Grand Marketplace level of the city, unless their work demanded it. Nia knew her parents would have absolute spasms if she suggested she might take a trip there. But she could find a way to get away with it. "Well, how can I claim to be a good palace guard if I can't face a little danger?" Nia asked. "Besides, I would love to know what this secret job is!"

"That's the Nia I know." Cephan moved closer and leaned in to kiss her cheek. Nia felt the water around them warming up considerably. Cephan had kissed her— finally! She almost forgot the disappointment of last night in the excitement of this moment.

He pulled back, staying within inches of her. "Meet me this evening, next to the pearl shop in the market," he told her, his hands still cupping her face. "You can tell your parents you need to buy something to wear to the celebration party after the Trials. I'll guide you from there."

Nia nodded, and then she became aware of a soft, high-pitched cry coming from all the little Farworlders. She moved out of Cephan's grasp and turned to stare at them. "What's wrong with them?" she asked, confused.

"Can't you tell? I am receiving a mental image now—

they are upset by seeing their favorite nanny so close with someone else," Cephan joked. Cephan was one of the few friends to whom Nia had revealed her secret, and even he teased her about it.

"Oh, stop!" Nia said. "Go, and I'll meet you later."

Cephan gave her a heart-melting smile. "I'll be waiting." He turned and swam away with powerful grace. The turbulent eddies his tail made in the water swirled around her, tantalizing her skin.

Nia watched him go, envious that he would be in the Trials, and realizing that it meant she probably wouldn't see him much for a while. Was that why he was choosing now to kiss her and to reveal parts of his life she hadn't known about before? Was he worried that it was their last chance to be close before he'd be too caught up in a new life? Nia shook her head. Her mother would say that she was "searching for stones in a pearl shop" and that she should stop it at once. She and Cephan had been getting closer all the time lately, and this was the natural next step. In fact, if he did become an Avatar, maybe he would even want her to become his . . .

The wailing of the infant Farworlders became impossible to ignore. Nia swam among them. "What is it? What is it?" she kept asking. But, of course, they couldn't tell her.

All their food bags were full, all their sand beds were sound. Nia couldn't imagine what was wrong. Sometimes mermyd infants became cranky for no reason—could it be the same for a Farworlder? *Maybe playing with Cephan's glass sphere tired them out, or they want to play with it more, that's all,* she thought. *But why won't they go to sleep? I could be training, like Garun, instead of being stuck here listening to this noise. Why wasn't I chosen for the Trials?*

Chapter Three

"Go," Nia said, slapping the dolphin messenger gently on the tail. The dolphin eagerly swam away, Nia's message to Callimar clutched between its teeth. Then Nia slipped out through a window. She had left a kelp note for the servants to tell her parents she would miss dinner with them, as she had gone to the market to meet Callimar. Nia hoped Callimar would agree that they had indeed gone to the marketplace together this evening, if anyone asked. Nia's parents generally didn't concern themselves much with her whereabouts, however, as long as she arrived home by a reasonable time. They were always too caught up in their own activities.

Nia swam through back alleys from her home near the Bluefin Palace to the market district. She hoped no one she knew would see her and wondered if she should have worn some sort of disguise. This sneaking around was hard, but Nia had to do this. She was so eager to see Cephan and to know what his secret was.

Light streamed from the windows of other clan palaces as celebrations continued for their chosen representatives in the Trials. Nia swam past the mother-of-pearl–faced palace of the Seabass and the black basalt fortress of the Orca, hearing music and laughter and cries of congratulations. She was so envious she could almost cry. But as Cephan told her once, the sea does not need more salt water, and so she held back her tears.

The Grand Marketplace of Atlantis was in the very center of the city, at midlevel. Buildings were constructed on top of older buildings, since Atlantis could not expand outward. History seemed alive in the Marketplace, because it still had some of the colonnaded porticos and mosaic stone plazas from the ancient days, when Atlantis was on the surface and land-dwellers walked among mermyds.

The Marketplace was full of exotic mystery, as well. Colorful booths made from silk draperies that had been retrieved from sunken ships could be found there. These booths often sold items from the land-dwellers' world, things impossible to make in undersea Atlantis—glass bottles, fired clay pots and bowls, steel knives, cloth of all sorts, some already sewn into garments, jewelry of gold and silver and precious stones. Many of these things rotted or rusted not long after being recovered, which often made them more costly and all the more fashionable.

During the hours of business, one could meet everyone and anyone in the Grand Marketplace. It was the heart of the city, which was why it was natural that Nia could encounter Cephan there.

It was late for business hours, however, and as Nia swam down into the Marketplace, she noted there were few people. Less of a crowd to hide in.

The recent fashion was to have booths in the shape of giant clam shells—which made opening and closing them for security quite simple. But this evening, most of the booths were closed, giving the Marketplace the appearance of a sleepy tide-pool. The pearl-seller was still open, but the owner was preparing to close up and was warily eyeing the one mermyd perusing her display.

Nia recognized the mermyd bending over the display table—it was Cephan, of course. As Nia came up beside him, he turned and said, "Here she is! I told you she'd be along soon."

The pearl-seller grunted, eyes narrowed.

"Cephan?"

"Listen, my love, I think Gathos has a better selection, don't you? These are too flawed, too dark. Perhaps I'd consider them if they had a bit more luster. Or a more reasonable price. Come along, darling, let's look someplace else." Cephan took Nia by the arm and, with powerful strokes of his tail, led her away. Behind them, the pearl-seller slammed her shop shut.

"What was that about?" Nia asked, wrinkling her nose in confusion.

"Well, I had to have some reason to be loitering around her booth—so many merchants think we bottom-dwellers have no money and are just wasting their time. So I told her that I was searching for a troth-token for my beloved. I don't think she believed me until you swam up."

Nia couldn't help wonder whether Cephan really did think of her as his beloved. She could barely keep her gills from fluttering at the thought. "Why wouldn't anyone believe you? You are the chosen of your clan," she said.

"But how would she know what I was?" he asked.

"It just seems that all the clans are shouting the names of their winners from their highest towers."

"I'm sure that can't be music to your ears," Cephan sympathized. "Especially hearing Garun's name. Well, the Stingrays aren't quite so vocal, I guess."

He led Nia to a weighted drapery that ran along the back of a little-used plaza. Pulling aside the drapery,

Cephan revealed a wall, at the top of which were small, square windows from which bubbles spewed merrily. "Do you know where we are?"

"Yes," Nia said. "These are the oxygenation tunnels that aerate the water that goes down into the—"

"Into the Lower Depths. Exactly." Cephan positioned himself before a metal door in the wall. Carved in the stone above the door were the words BEWARE—DO NOT ENTER—WORKERS ONLY. Cephan reached into a depression in the door and turned a scallop-shaped knob.

"Cephan, what are you doing?" Nia cried. "These tunnels are dangerous!"

"It's all right. I'm a worker." He flashed a brief smile. "Now. We must be quick. Hang on to me, tight as you can, no matter what." Cephan grasped Nia's arms and pulled them around his waist. With his left hand he shoved the door open, and then he swam in, pulling Nia in with him.

It was pitch dark inside, and the current in the tunnel was tremendously swift, sucking them downward. Nia felt her arms slipping from Cephan's waist. Cephan grabbed onto a metal rung in the side of the tunnel and held her close. The bubbling water roared past Nia's ears, and she hung on to Cephan with every muscle. It would have been more romantic if she hadn't been so terrified.

"Breathe!" Cephan yelled in her ear. "Open your gills and breathe!"

Nia's gills had closed with fear, but she tentatively let them open—and then the swift water forced them open, shoving superoxygenated water through them. Within seconds, Nia felt energized, more awake than she'd been her entire life. Her fingers and toes began to tingle. Her eyes opened wide.

"That should be enough," Cephan said. "Now hold your breath. We're going for a ride, and the speed could make it hard to take in air properly." He let go of the rung, and suddenly the two of them were carried headlong down the tunnel, racing with the swift flowing water.

This was a greater thrill than the currents she had ridden around the rim of Atlantis as a child. The tunnel dipped downward, and they plummeted toward the ocean floor. It bent horizontal again, and they zoomed along faster than any mermyd could swim. It was wonderful . . . until Nia realized she was beginning to run out of breath.

They stopped, jarringly, as Cephan caught another rung on the side of the tunnel. "Time to breathe again!"

Nia opened her gills again and felt her head go light as the bubbling water rushed in. She noticed, now that her eyes had adjusted, that there were dim phosphorescent glows spaced evenly along the tunnel. One was right over Cephan's head, marking where the rung was. *So that's how he can find them*. Her heart was pounding in her chest, and her limbs were shaking.

"Ready to go again?" Cephan asked.

"I think I'm getting dizzy."

"That's normal. Enjoy it. One more run, and then we're there. Ready? Here we go." Cephan let go of the rung, and the water took them again.

This time, Nia found the headlong rush pleasant, as the swift water spun her and Cephan around and around. They held each other tightly. The bubbles roared in her ears and sang in her bloodstream. Her skin felt like it was humming. Her fears temporarily vanished in the overwhelming sound and sensation.

It all ended with a jerk as Cephan grabbed another rung. "Whoa, I nearly missed our stop. Hang on." He let go of her to use both hands to open a door. Nia's hands started to slip from his waist again, but Cephan caught her arm just in time and pulled her through. As she went through the door, Nia noticed a different phosphorescent marking above the doorway, larger than those above the rungs. *Aha. And that's how he finds a door.*

Cephan slammed the access door shut behind them.

The normal water outside the tunnel seemed so still and quiet, it was eerie. It took her gills some moments to adjust to regular breathing. "Amazing!" was all she could say. Then she noticed a strange, mineral, fishy taste to the water and made a face. "What *is* it that I'm tasting?"

"Well, we don't have the freshest water down here in the Lower Depths. But we like to say, 'Our water may be thicker, but it has more flavor.'"

"I . . . see. Or taste, rather."

"No time to hang around. This way." Cephan took her arm again and led her along a dim corridor that had clearly not been meant for public travel. The walls were bare, undressed stone, and pipes ran along the ceiling.

As they progressed, Nia felt the water getting warmer. It gently pulsated around her. She heard a low, distant thrumming, deep as a whale-song, but more regular. "What is that sound? And why does the water feel so strange?"

"We're getting nearer the engines that drive most of the works of Atlantis. Just below us, on the ocean floor, there is a great rift with powerful steam vents shooting out of it."

"I remember learning about those vents in Early Academy," Nia said. "The rift is a great crack in the earth that splits the seabed in two. Some say it goes all the way through the world. It bleeds liquid stone, heating the sea around it and adding minerals to the water that keep us healthy."

"You were a good student," Cephan said. "But the vents do more than just heat the water. The steam and hot water that comes out of the geysers is so fast and powerful that it can drive the great engines that run the filtration and aeration tunnels of the city. Of course, the works are primitive compared to what the Farworlders were used to on their planet, but it's better than anything the land-dwellers have."

Nia stared at Cephan in surprise. "I'd always thought it was the Council's telekinetic magic that kept things running. How do you know so much about the Farworlders and the land-dwellers?"

Cephan grinned. "I told you about my cousin—he knows about the land-dwellers. As for the Farworlders and the Councils . . . well, you'll find out in a minute. This way." He led her up a sloping tunnel to the right and opened a door at the end of the tunnel.

The plaza they swam out onto was almost a mirror of the Great Marketplace, only smaller and more cluttered. Here there were booths built from old masts or ship timbers and covered with ropy fishnet or sailcloth instead of silk. The taste of fish, seaweed, scallops, and shrimp on the water was nearly overwhelming. It reminded Nia that she had skipped dinner.

Mermyds bustled back and forth with baskets full of shellfish and wrapped filets and bunches of seaweed, shooing away the clouds of little fish that nipped at the baskets, hoping for a stray morsel. Other mermyds swam past carrying spears and lanterns that glowed with a red light.

"Welcome to our market," Cephan said. "This is where the kelp farmers and the hunters bring in their harvest. The hunters carry those red lanterns because the deep-sea fish can't see red light. This means the hunters can see their prey, but the hunters are invisible to the fish. It makes their work pretty easy."

"I never knew that," Nia marveled.

"Over there," Cephan went on, pointing to a group of mermyds with masks over their mouths and cloth filters over their gills, "they take what has rotted or cannot be sold, shred it, and pipe it out to sea. The pipes go out a long way before the refuse is released into the water. Otherwise it would just come back in through the filtration tubes. We once had a blowout in a refuse pipe near my tube about a year ago. It was nasty. And the sharks hanging around to feed just outside the Dome weren't any fun either."

"I hadn't realized things were so . . . exciting down here," Nia said.

"Well, now you know," he said with a smile. "Why

don't you wait over there for a minute? There's something I have to do."

Nia went over to the pile of empty baskets and rope that Cephan pointed to and hovered beside it, feeling very conspicuous. But the mermyds of the Lower Depths paid her little attention, going about their business as if she weren't there, except for a grizzled old fish-seller who winked at her flirtatiously.

Nia pointedly ignored him and kept her eyes on Cephan, who was talking to a farmer at one of the fishnet-covered booths. The farmer handed Cephan two small baskets. Cephan then swam back to Nia, motioning her to follow him.

"Are we going on a picnic in the Kelp Orchard?"

"Um, the food is not for us, I'm afraid. This is all about that responsibility of mine, remember?"

"Oh, you're the keeper of the city's sea turtles!" Nia teased.

It was amusing to see Cephan try to scowl and smile at the same time. "Lady Niniane, how am I ever going to impress you when you think such things of me?"

"But that *would* be a big responsibility. The elderly merfolk need the turtles to carry them around when they can't swim so well anymore. And the children—"

"It's an even *bigger* responsibility than that," Cephan interrupted. "Much bigger," he added.

"Oh. Well, then. Please lead on," Nia said, smiling.

Cephan led her out of the lower market, back down into the access tunnel. Instead of swimming back to the oxygenation tunnel, though, he turned right. The access tunnel descended even deeper below the city. The water became thicker, with a stronger mineral taste, and the temperature grew even warmer.

The walls of the tunnel were more and more moss covered as they progressed, and here and there colonies of red tube worms had anchored themselves to the stone. Tiny fish and deep-sea shrimp fed among the moss, their biochemical lights glowing and glimmering.

"Doesn't anyone clean down here?" asked Nia. Her good mood was being replaced by a disquieting sense of foreboding.

"The scrubbing crew comes around every few years," said Cephan. "But the stuff grows back right away. These tunnels don't get much traffic, anyway."

"I see," Nia said. "So your responsibility doesn't involve housekeeping."

"No," Cephan said with a quick smile. "Be patient. We're almost there."

The throbbing in the water now echoed in Nia's chest, and her gills were having to work harder than usual. "Cephan? I don't mean to complain, but this is becoming uncomfortable."

"Peace. We're here." Cephan stopped in front of a huge, circular door with an iron wheel in its center.

"What is it?" Nia asked.

"It's the heart of the works of Atlantis," Cephan said, his voice deepening. "It's also a prison. And I am the jailer."

Chapter Four

"A . . . prison?" Nia stopped still in the water. Prisons and dungeons were a barbarity practiced by the land-dwellers. Every Atlantean was taught that in Academy. Those of violent or antisocial mind in Atlantis were given community tasks to help them reform. Severe crimes were almost unheard of in Atlantis, but those who committed them were banished from the city. Being trapped in one room, even with moving water, was terrifying to a mermyd. "Are you joking, Cephan? Atlantis doesn't have a prison. We . . . we don't need one."

"We needed this one. And there are just two prisoners."

"Who? Why?"

"In a moment, you'll see." Cephan handed her the two baskets and then withdrew a key from behind a patch of moss. After inserting it into a tiny hole on the side of the wheel, he turned the wheel with a mighty pull.

"You mean, someone is locked up in one room, in this awful place?" Nia asked, the water feeling cold around her.

There was a clack as the round door unlocked, and Cephan swung it open. "Prison is for punishment, Nia, and punishment is not intended to be pleasant."

"Punishment?" Nia had difficulty with the word. Punishment was for children; being sent to one's room to stay for a short period of time, or being forbidden a treat if one disobeyed one's elders. What adult mermyd would have merited punishment rather than healing?

Cephan swam through the opening and motioned for Nia to follow. She did so, but reluctantly.

The water was a little cooler just beyond the round door, but the thrumming was, if anything, louder. As Nia's eyes adjusted, she could see they were in a narrow room. Across from the door was a low wall, about waist height if her feet were on the floor. A few strands of wire crossed the upper opening.

Beyond the low wall was an amazing chamber whose gleaming metal walls were covered with knobs and levers and glowing diagrams. Through a window on the far side of the chamber, she could glimpse great wheels turning and pistons and bellows moving back and forth.

"What *is* all that?" Nia asked softly.

"Farworlder technology," replied Cephan. "I don't claim to understand it, but it brings up the warm water from the rift, cleanses it, and sends it through the city's tunnels and pipes. It's what keeps our water moving and fresh."

"And prisoners are kept *here*?"

"As atonement. The Councils felt the prisoners ought to have meaningful and important tasks to do. And that's all I should tell you." Cephan reached up and touched one of the wires that crossed the water in front of them. For a second there was a horrible, high-pitched squeal through the water. "I am here!" Cephan called out.

A mermyd of middle years swam into view from behind the low wall Nia had seen. He had black-and-silver hair and a neatly trimmed dark beard streaked with gray. The scales of his tail fin were silvery black. With dignified slowness, he came up to the wall. "You're late."

Cephan simply nodded.

"And you've brought a guest," the mermyd added, gazing at Nia with intense interest.

"She's from the Farworlder palace guard, here for observation," Cephan lied.

"Ah. I see. Come to take note of your procedure, has she?" he asked, sounding amused.

Nia tried to give him a stern, official-seeming nod. Inside, she was reeling from everything she had seen.

Still staring at her, the prisoner went on, "The Bluefins have always produced such strikingly unique individuals."

"How did you . . ." Nia began, but stopped herself. *Did I already give something away I shouldn't have?*

"I see traces of Dyonis in you," the prisoner explained. "Back in earlier, better days, I made a study of mermyd bloodlines."

Cephan loudly cleared his throat and said, "Here is your dinner." He slipped the baskets through the narrow space between the wires.

The prisoner reached up to catch them, and Nia saw the sun-shaped scar on his right palm. Her heart nearly stopped. "You . . . you are an Avatar!" she blurted out.

"She doesn't know?" the prisoner asked Cephan, raising an eyebrow.

"You know I'm not allowed to talk about you to others," Cephan replied carefully. "Not even to the palace guard."

"Ah. Indeed I was, young lady," the prisoner replied. "But that was a long time ago." He caught the baskets before they drifted to the floor. Unfolding the cloth cover on one of them, he remarked, "Ah, crab cakes. My favorite."

"It's what you get every day," Cephan said.

"Then it's good that they're my favorite, yes?"

"Who *are* you?" Nia asked, unable to stop herself. She had never heard of an Avatar being imprisoned—the idea was shocking, inconceivable. It was as though a wall in a very familiar room in her house had crumbled away, revealing a dark unknown chamber.

"Is this a test?" the prisoner asked with a baffled smile. "As my keeper has already no doubt informed you, I'm not permitted to tell you my name, or even why I'm here. It's part of my punishment." He winked at her and stuffed a crab cake into his mouth.

"If you are . . . *were* an Avatar, where is your—" Before Nia could finish the sentence, she heard movement from the direction where the prisoner had come from. She glanced over at the wall in time to see a Farworlder swimming around it, coming toward them. It was as long as a mermyd, with head and tentacles a deep purple in color, and huge golden eyes. It flowed through the water as if made of liquid itself, a supple shadow, a sentient stain. It reached into the basket the prisoner was holding and deftly snatched out a crab cake for itself.

"You were saying?" the prisoner asked.

"Never mind," Nia breathed. She was grateful for the wall that stood between them. While Farworlder infants were delicate and weak, adult Farworlders were immensely strong. Even a casual flick from a Farworlder's tentacle could leave severe bruising. The full-force grip of a Farworlder's tentacle could crush a mermyd's bones. It was said that this was why Farworlders chose to live apart from mermyds other than Avatars. And another reason only the strongest and healthiest mermyds were chosen to become Avatars. Nia had always tried to ignore the small bit of fear she'd had of Farworlders, since she knew it was necessary in order to become an Avatar. She was sure that once she'd connected with one in the Naming ceremony, any fear she had would fade. But right now, she could barely remember to keep her gills open and breathe.

Suddenly she became aware that the Farworlder was staring at her. Nia felt her skin creep as she felt its touch on her mind. It was very different from the tickle of the infant Farworlder in the nursery. This was subtle, yet powerful, reaching deep into her thoughts. Nia swallowed hard, forcing down her fear.

It became worse when the mermyd prisoner stared as well, his eyes narrowed, weighing her, gauging her. Nia was getting the strange sense that this ex-Avatar and his king considered her *important*. She wasn't even sure what that meant, but the thought was there in her head.

Nia balled her fists at her sides and let her gills flare to pull in more oxygen from the water. She let one thought fill her mind, not knowing if the Farworlder would read it. *Whatever it is you are trying to get from me, you cannot have it,* she thought, staring back hard at the creature.

The ex-Avatar prisoner raised his brows in surprise, and a slight smile appeared on his lips. "Well, well," he said. "The Bluefins remain a remarkable family." He inclined his head to her as if bowing.

"Nia, are you all right?" Cephan asked, gently touching her arm.

"I believe I've seen enough," Nia said, still trying to sound official. "I wish to go now."

"Yes, of course." Cephan glared at the prisoner, who, if anything, looked even more amused. Cephan spun the iron wheel in the door and opened it, guiding Nia through.

"A pleasure to have met you, Lady Nia," the prisoner called after them before Cephan shut the great round door behind them.

In a flash of anger sparked by fear, Nia burst out, "Should you have said my *name* in front of him?"

Cephan grasped her shoulders. "I'm so sorry, it just slipped out. *Are* you all right?"

"Yes, I think so. That . . . Farworlder . . . don't laugh, Cephan, but I felt that creature touch my mind, just like the infant in the nursery."

"I won't laugh," Cephan said quite seriously. "But he didn't harm you?"

"No." Nia reached up and ran her hands across her scalp, through her hair. "No, I was able to hold him off. In my thoughts, I mean."

Cephan paused and stared at her. "No wonder he was impressed."

"Cephan, who *is* he? And who is the Farworlder with him?"

Cephan shook his head sadly. "Rules are rules, Nia. I can't speak their names or their crimes. I shouldn't have even brought you here."

"Crimes?" Nia repeated. "Did they do something very bad?"

"I don't know, and even if I did I couldn't tell you."

"Why is someone who did something bad put in charge of the water flow of Atlantis?" she asked, incredulous. It didn't make any sense.

"Oh, they aren't in charge, and it would be noticed right away if they tried to stop the machinery," Cephan explained. "They can't do any damage on their own.

They were given worthwhile work to do as part of their atonement."

"It's because he was an Avatar that they had to imprison him, isn't it?" Nia pressed. "He and his king could resist the healing of the High Council, or . . . or maybe he chose this punishment instead of healing so that the High Council couldn't read his thoughts."

Cephan's eyes opened wide but he shrugged. "I'm sorry, but I really can't tell you."

"But you did bring me here, and as you said, you shouldn't have even done that."

He looked down at the floor. "I'm sorry. I wanted . . . I wanted you to see that I have an important position too. I'm the jailer for the only prisoners in Atlantis. I bring the food, make sure the cell water is clean. I check to make sure there are no unusual changes to the equipment and the alarm wires haven't been tampered with. But I can't talk about it with anyone. Still, I—I hated to have such a big secret from you," he admitted, raising his gaze to meet hers again.

Nia smiled, staring back into his eyes for a moment. "How long have the prisoners been down here?" she couldn't resist asking.

Cephan laughed. "No more questions, all right? You

have to promise me that you won't tell anyone I brought you here or that you have seen these prisoners. I might lose my chance to be in the Trials, or worse, if anyone found out."

"All right, I promise," Nia said, worrying that a heavy burden had just been placed on her shoulders.

"I know. I trust you." Cephan smiled. "I'd better be getting you back upstairs," he said. "You'll have less to explain to your family if you're in early."

"Can't we be together just a little while longer?" Nia asked, frowning. "You could show me where you live."

Cephan smiled regretfully. "It will take you a while to get back up to your home level. We can't go back the way we came—the oxygenation tunnels flow only one way. Besides, I ought to go train a bit for the Trials. I may not have much hope of winning, but at least I can make a good effort."

"How can you say that?" Nia asked. "I'm glad *I* won't be competing against you in the racing Trials, and I don't see how anyone else could do much better than me."

Cephan blushed. "But I have little training in the magical and mental arts," he said. "Those of us in the Toiling clans do not have the time for it that your clan does. That's where I may fall behind."

"Well, you don't have to win every Trial to be deemed

worthy of Ascension to Avatar." Nia squeezed his hand to reassure him.

"But it helps," Cephan answered with a grin. "Now come on. We don't want your parents sending out search dolphins for you." He guided her back through the mossy tunnels, up to the Lower Market. Again, no one took much notice of them, as the merchants and farmers were closing up their booths.

Cephan led Nia over to one thin, wiry merchant who was piling fish into large baskets that were attached to a vertical rope. "Excuse me, Spyridon," Cephan said, "by any chance are you sending dinners to the upper houses? If so, I've something else for you to deliver." Cephan put a small pearl in the merchant's hand and then gestured toward Nia.

"Hmm." Spyridon hefted the pearl, examined it closely, and then narrowed his eyes at Nia. "Is he too tight-fisted to get you a turtle-taxi?"

"Not at all," Nia protested.

"It's just that it would be too slow," Cephan said. "She needs to be home by a certain time."

"Ah," Spyridon said with an understanding nod and a grin. "I'll agree to it, if you'll help with the hauling."

"Seems only fair," Cephan said.

So Spyridon hauled on the rope until an empty basket was on the floor. Nia stepped in and curled up. "This goes up to the Starfish warehouse," the merchant explained. "You know where that is?"

"Oh, yes, that's not far from my home."

"Good. Say hello to Vilus for me. I'd love to see the expression on his face when he finds *you* in a basket instead of fish."

"I will," Nia said. "Thank you." She turned to smile at Cephan. "Will I see you again soon?" she asked in a low voice.

"You'll see me in the Trials," he responded.

"Well, yes," Nia said, her smile fading. "But that's not the same thing."

"I'll get away from the training for a little while, if I can," Cephan promised.

"Hey, hey!" Spyridon said, interrupting them. "I want to be closing up now."

Nia let Cephan close the basket lid over her. The weave of the basket was open enough that she could peer out and watch as Cephan and Spyridon hauled on the rope, raising Nia's basket and the others higher and higher.

Unfortunately, the slow ascent gave Nia too much time to think. The meeting with the prisoner Avatar and his

Farworlder king had unnerved her. They had stared at her with such intensity. *I felt as though they knew who I was. Or have they been so long without company that any visitor is important?* The touch of the Farworlder's mind was frightening, as if the alien creature had been searching for something in her thoughts.

But what? Nia wondered. *If only there was someone I could ask. But it's bad enough how no one believes me about the baby Farworlder. If I were to claim an adult Farworlder tried to join thoughts with mine . . .* Nia rubbed her arms. The water was cooler as her basket rose farther out of the Lower Depths, but she did not think that was the only reason for the chill she felt.

Chapter Five

Nia lazily followed the Academy instructor around the circular room, hanging back in the school of mermyd students that swam in the instructor's wake. It was important to keep moving in an Academy classroom; otherwise it would be all too tempting to fall asleep. The idea that a subject could be deadly dull was more than just a figure of speech to a mermyd.

Her instructor, Master Zale, was the fishiest mermyd Nia had ever known. His eyes were huge and set wide apart. His face was long and narrow, and a finned ear stuck out from each side of his head. *Now if he had a fin on the back and top of his head*, Nia thought, *he would scarcely need a body at all.*

"We are most fortunate," burbled Master Zale, "in having the important events of the upcoming weeks to witness and discuss. The opportunity to see an Ascension will be invaluable to your understanding of the politics and history of Atlantis. As you witness the Trials and come to understand their purpose, you will gain insight as to how Atlantean government came to be the way it is, and why it is the best system for serving our citizens."

It had been two days since Nia had last seen Cephan. She hoped his training was going well, and that he hadn't gotten into trouble for taking her to see the prisoners. Nia's surprise appearance in the Starfish warehouse had delighted some of the workers there, and severely annoyed the overseer. Nia hadn't gotten into any trouble, though, even when the officious overseer had insisted on taking Nia home and personally complaining to her parents. Tyra and Pontus had only sighed and told Nia she didn't have to pull such pranks in order to get attention, and could she please behave herself while they went to her aunt and uncle's home to help with Garun. Strangely, they hadn't invited her to join them. In fact, they'd made it quite clear they didn't intend for her to come, giving her a silly excuse for why she should stay behind. Apparently they just wanted to focus their complete attention on Garun.

Garun, Garun, Garun. That was all she was hearing around her relatives lately. Nia was getting the impression Garun was not doing well in some of his training. Part of her felt smug, and she wanted to shout at them, *See? You should have chosen me!* But Nia knew that wouldn't make any difference. So rather than stay at home and mope on a day when she didn't have work at the nursery, Nia went to the Academy.

Classes were informal in Atlantis after childhood— students could come to the Academy whenever they liked to hear lectures or use the library. Certain classes, such as mathematics or rhetoric, required attendance several days in a row. But this was political history, and Nia could easily just wander in to listen for a while.

"As you have no doubt heard, each of the seven Trials," Master Zale droned on as he wriggled around the room, "tests for a particular virtue prized in an Avatar. The First Trial, a swimming race, tests for overall health of the body. The Second Trial tests for will and stamina, as well as health. The Third Trial tests cleverness and teamwork. The Fourth and Fifth test problem solving and wisdom. The Sixth tests one's connection to the numinous, one's magic. And the last, of course, is the Riddle, which tests the ability to think creatively. No mermyd can excel at all of these, of course, which is why the Trials are a slow process of elimination."

"Excuse me, Master Zale," Nia asked, "does this mean that if a mermyd does badly on, say, any two of the Trials, he might still have a chance for Ascension?"

Master Zale turned his head and regarded Nia with his enormous eyes. "Ah. Lady Niniane, isn't it? Of the Bluefin Clan?"

All the other students turned to look at her, and Nia felt like a fish caught in a net. "Um . . . yes, sir."

"Well. I can understand your concerns," Master Zale said. "You are thinking of your clan's candidate, are you not? An interesting choice, he was. But no, circumstances do not change, young lady. Your candidate must not be among the six poorest in the field. If he is eliminated, for example, in the first two Trials, he cannot hope to become the Avatar." Master Zale continued to address the class. "In this way, imperfections are avoided, and only those who are truly worthy are allowed to Ascend. The citizens of Atlantis are therefore guaranteed that their government is of the finest mermyds who will never falter or misuse their power."

Something rang false in the instructor's words. *If the Avatars are only the finest mermyds*, Nia thought, *then why is one of them imprisoned in the Lower Depths?*

"You mean to say a mistake has never been made in choosing an Avatar?" Nia blurted out.

Zale blinked at her and rubbed his nose. "Never."

"No one has ever been forced to step down from the Council? They leave *only* by retirement?"

Master Zale's pale-green face began to flush an ugly blue. "Young lady, I don't know what you intend by this line of argument. But it is as I have said. Atlanteans may put their full and complete trust in the High and Low Councils. The Farworlders would permit nothing less." Then Master Zale turned his back on her and continued on with his lecture.

He didn't deny it outright, Nia realized. *So maybe he knew about the prisoners. But just like Cephan, he's not allowed to say anything.* Nia felt as though she'd just learned something far more important than all the dry facts in Zale's lecture. *Atlantis is not quite the perfect and open place it seems, if there are truths people dare not talk about.* Nia swam along silently at the back of the school, pretending to pay rapt attention to everything Master Zale said.

"When an Avatar is selected in the Trials," the lecturer went on, "we then proceed to the Naming. No one knows the origins of this ritual, or who the first pairing of Avatar and Farworlder might have been. There are some here at the Academy who accept that Poseidonis was the first, but that is under dispute. It is known that the Farworlders, upon reaching Earth's ocean, chose from the native land-dwellers individuals with latent magical abilities similar and complementary to their own. From these chosen land-dwellers, the Farworlders created the mermyd race to live beside them in the sea."

He's straying a bit from politics and government, Nia noticed. *Maybe to distract everyone from the questions I asked.*

"Perhaps it was accident," Zale went on, "that one day a Farworlder struck a mermyd with its taloned tentacle and thereby injected the toxins of its oculus into the mermyd's blood. Perhaps it was accident that the two beings thus joined discovered they had enhanced mental and magical powers. Or perhaps it was what the Farworlders had intended all along—"

"Master Zale?" piped up a young mermyd. "Master Zale, I learned in Fish Studies that all parts of an animal have a purpose. But if the tentacle with talons wasn't originally for joining with mermyds, what do the Farworlders use it for?"

Master Zale slowly turned a deeper shade of blue. Other student mermyds quietly giggled. Master Zale cleared his throat and said, "Assuming your question is serious, I am given to understand that the tentacle has use during . . . mating rituals."

The giggles got louder. Master Zale glared around the room. "And out of respect for our wise and noble Farworlders, that is all I will say on *that* subject."

As the laughter subsided, Nia felt some relief, and some gratitude toward the young mermyd. *Maybe now Master Zale will forget my questions. At least I'm not the most annoying student he has today.*

Another mermyd, who wore the bright magenta and yellow colors of the Anemone Clan, spoke up. "Master Zale, about the Naming—my mother tells me she's glad I wasn't chosen as the candidate for our family. She said the Naming could be dangerous, and I could die. Is that true?"

Master Zale blinked and folded his hands in front of him. "I am sure your mother loves you very much, young sir. But I am pleased to say you may inform her she is in error. While there are theoretical hazards, the ritual and the Trials have been developed, over centuries, to ensure that the danger to both Farworlder and Avatar is minimal. First of all, as you would be aware, had you been listening earlier, only the healthiest of mermyds is chosen to become an Avatar. Second, the entire mental concentration of both High and Low Councils, with all its healing capacity, is focused on the pair during the ritual. With such care taken, there is simply no opportunity for mishaps to occur."

Oh, he answered that carefully too, Nia noticed. He didn't say that no mermyd had ever died during the Naming.

"What exactly happens during the Naming that could be dangerous?" another mermyd asked. Nia recognized her as the chosen candidate for the Seabass Clan. *Well, I guess she has the right to ask. She might have to face the risk.*

Master Zale sighed and rolled his eyes. "We are getting a bit off topic here, but I suppose it is better that you be properly informed so that you do not make the wrong assumptions, like that young fellow's mother. Put simply, it is this: Before the Naming ritual begins, certain . . . preparations are done to increase the secretions of the oculus gland in the young Farworlder's bloodstream. This is toxic to the young Farworlder, and those secretions must be released within seven days, or the creature will die. That is one danger. These secretions are also poisonous to the Avatar, and if they were left in his or her bloodstream untransformed, the Avatar would also die in a number of days. That is another danger. Third, once mental joining is established, and it typically happens as soon as the talons of the Farworlder break the skin of the Avatar's hand, then should one of the pair die, the other will as well.

"*However*," Master Zale emphasized, "the whole *point* of the Naming ritual is that the healing magic, the mental concentration of the new Avatar and the Councils is focused on changing the secretion so that it is no longer toxic in either the Avatar or the new king. So, you see, there is no reason to fear the Ascension. While there may be moments of unpleasantness, there is no question that the Avatar chosen will come through the ritual whole and healthy."

"But what if one's blood is resistant to being changed by magic?" the Seabass mermyd persisted. She had clearly not been reassured by Master Zale's explanation.

"You have been talking to a physician or two, apparently," Master Zale said. "This person should have told you that a mermyd with such a condition, and that condition is very rare, would simply not have been chosen as a candidate. One whose blood resists magic would show certain odd qualities during magical training, and therefore it would be known well ahead of time."

Nia was now paying very close attention. *Is that it? Was I not chosen because I have this rare condition? I've been told my magical skills are strange.* This was something she'd have to ask Dyonis later.

"Why is the ritual called the Naming?" another mermyd asked.

Master Zale looked as though his patience was at an end. "Don't parents tell their offspring *anything* these days? As a sign that the ritual is complete and the joining safely accomplished, the Avatar announces to the assembly the name by which the Farworlder king wishes to be known. From that point on, the Avatar is able to speak for the Farworlder king and share its thoughts with the Councils and the citizens of Atlantis. Now, if we could *please* return to the discussion of history—"

A dolphin swam into the room, squeaking loudly, to signal that class was at an end.

Master Zale threw out his hands in exasperation. "It would appear fate is against me today. Those interested in learning more about the development of government may return tomorrow at the usual time."

Nia hoped she could leave inconspicuously. But she was at the opposite side of the room from the door when class ended, and the way was blocked by all the students ahead of her. She was unable to escape quite fast enough.

"*Lady Niniane!*" Master Zale called out. "If you would be so kind as to stay after for a moment."

Now I've done it, Nia thought with a sickening sinking of her stomach. *I've revealed I have hidden knowledge. Zale will go to my parents and Cephan will be punished and everything will fall apart.* "Yes, Master Zale?" she said, her voice cracking.

The instructor looked her over disapprovingly. "Well. I

suppose you've been hearing stories from your illustrious grandfather. That's Dyonis's right, if he wants to discuss such things within the family. But these things are not for public discourse, you understand? If you wish to talk about such things, you must do so with him.

"You see, Atlanteans *must* have trust in their government. Without it, we would be no better than the constantly warring land-dwellers. In any case, Dyonis should have taught you better than to speak of Ma'el in public. The law is the law. Do not refer even indirectly to him in these halls ever again, do you understand?"

Nia nodded. Her mind was racing, but she tried to appear calm. "Yes, Master Zale. I'm sorry. I won't do it again."

So the prisoner is called Ma'el, she thought with excitement. *If Master Zale thinks it's possible that Grandfather would talk to me about Ma'el, then Dyonis must know the truth. I'll have to talk to him, as soon as I can.* And then she would know the whole story.

Chapter Six

"You've arranged *what?*" Nia exclaimed around a mouthful of minced crab meat.

"Don't talk until you've swallowed, Nia," Pontus grumbled. "And be respectful. Goodness, I thought we'd raised you better than this."

Nia dutifully chewed and swallowed, determined to speak again at the first polite opportunity. She'd come home from the Academy expecting to have a quick, uninteresting dinner so that she could slip away to speak to Dyonis. And her parents chose that time to spring a surprise on her.

"Now, you understand it's not for certain," Tyra said, unable to contain a pleased-with-herself smile. "But I have spoken with the right people, and I think they were charmed with the thought of you taking over Garun's position at the Archives."

"But, Mother, I *enjoy* working in the nursery," Nia protested. *And I would be bored to tears working in the Archives*, she added to herself.

"Now, now, I remember how you complained when you first took that position," Tyra said, wagging a finger. "How you felt it wasn't a worthy place for you. The Archives is a much more prestigious Ministry in which to be employed. And a suitable place to use that fine, inquisitive mind of yours. From there, who knows where you might go? You could do research projects for the Academy, perhaps even teach there someday."

And become like Master Zale? Oh, no! "But—"

"Niniane!" Pontus interjected. "Your . . . Tyra has worked very hard to secure this position for you. It is a post that brings honor to the Bluefin Clan, and we would like to keep it within the Bluefin Clan after Garun leaves." He coughed. "Rather, *if* Garun leaves. Of course, we are all trying to think positively about his chances." He exchanged a glance with Tyra, then returned to his dinner.

Nia sighed. It seemed that every time her cousin's name came up lately, her parents acted stranger. Were they embarrassed to talk about him in front of Nia, since they knew she was upset over not being chosen herself? "I understand you're hoping for the, uh, for the best," Nia said carefully. "But if Garun *doesn't* become an Avatar, won't he want his position at the Archives back?"

"Garun will Ascend," Pontus growled, stabbing at his

crab meat roll with his eating trident. "Really, Nia, where is your family loyalty? I sometimes marvel that you are . . . descended from our great elder Dyonis."

Nia held very still. Every now and then, in her family, she felt an undercurrent of things not being said. Her parents would trail off and end their thoughts in strange ways. Lately it had been worse than ever. Dyonis was the only one who seemed to hold nothing back from her. And she hoped that would hold true when she asked him about Ma'el.

Tyra reached over and squeezed Pontus's arm. "No need for such harshness, dear. Nia is merely concerned on Garun's behalf. But, Nia, you really should be thinking of your own future, now that you aren't going to become an Avatar yourself."

Nia could see this was one argument she simply wasn't going to win. Perhaps she would not have to stay in the Archives long, once they discovered she was unsuitable for it. Maybe that was another thing she could ask Dyonis—if there was some way she could avoid working in the Archives. Maybe he'd know of some other eminent post that she could take that would please her parents as much if not more. "Yes, Mother. You're right. I'm sorry. I ought to be thinking about my future." *But not necessarily the future you plan for me.*

"That's better," Tyra said. "You see, Pontus. I told you she'd come around."

"Hmm," Pontus said, sounding unconvinced.

Nia was silent for a while, concentrating on her dinner, trying to settle into a comfortable reclining position on her dining couch. This dining in a formal setting, attaching oneself to one piece of furniture while eating off little tables, was a land-dweller custom picked up by mermyds in the time before the Sinking. It didn't make sense to Nia—she would just as soon eat and swim. But her parents appreciated the old ways. Nia remembered hearing stories about how, before the Sinking, there were wild mermyds who lived much of their life out in the open ocean and who would catch their meals and eat, just like any other sea creature. While the thought of biting into a still-wriggling fish was rather disgusting, Nia found the freedom of such a life attractive.

If such wild mermyds existed, Nia wondered, *what happened to them after the Sinking? Maybe that's another thing I could ask Dyonis.* Nia watched her parents eat and thought about mentioning her intention to visit her grandfather, but hesitated. The mood in the room was strange tonight, and while Nia couldn't think of a reason why they might forbid her to see her own grandfather, she wouldn't put it past them to come up with one. Nia needed to speak to Dyonis too much to risk it.

Finally, her parents finished eating. Tyra struck a chime beside her dining couch, and Sala, their housemaid, who was of the Shrimp Clan, came in and cleared dishes away.

With a couple of flaps of his arms and tail, Pontus raised his girth from his couch. "We are off to see to Garun again," he announced to Nia. "But your, uh, your presence won't be needed there. Try not to get into trouble while we're gone."

Nia forced herself to smile. "I won't."

"You might begin thinking," Tyra said, "of what you will say to the Master of Archives when I arrange an interview with him for you. You want to be sure to make a good impression."

"I will," Nia promised. "Wish Garun good luck for me."

"He won't be needing luck," Pontus grumbled. Again, Tyra touched his arm, concern in her face.

Why is Father so on edge? Nia wondered. She decided to make a graceful exit before she set him off further. "Of course. Have a good evening. I'll just be in my room, reading." She swam off to her sleeping chamber.

Mermyd homes, by tradition as well as necessity, were built rather like the structure of a coral reef. Each clan had its palace, and individual families' homes branched off from the palace. Each branch was a series of connected rooms. Because of the need to keep water flowing, there were very few solid doors in a mermyd home. Sometimes cloth would be used to cover entryways, and windows would be covered with a fine mesh net to keep out the occasional inquisitive dolphin, sea turtle, or mermyd child. But this meant that privacy was a rare thing in mermyd life. So Nia had to actually go into her sleep chamber, nestle onto her hammock of silken cord net, take up her kelpaper journal, and pretend to read until she was certain her parents had left the family branch.

When Nia felt secure that they were gone, she undid the netting on the window and slipped out.

Dyonis, as befitting his rank as elder and former Avatar, had the entire uppermost floor of the Bluefin Palace as his residence. Ordinarily, visitors would enter his dwelling by way of a swimwell within the palace itself. But Nia, ever since childhood, had always entered through the north window, and Dyonis had never seemed to mind. It was a long swim up—Nia was not one of those mermyds so skilled at getting oxygen out of the water that she could levitate using air in her lungs. But she did not mind the exercise. And the view from on high, near the crest of the Dome, was spectacular. The whole city glittered below her.

Sure enough, the north window was unnetted. And when Nia swam in, she was greeted by the smiling head butler, Keril of the Ramora Clan, who was dressed in an elegant pearl-gray tunic. "Ah, Lady Niniane. We have been expecting you."

"You have?" Nia had known Keril almost as long as she'd known Dyonis, and she felt as comfortable with him as she did with her grandfather. "He's not mad at me, is he? For the way I've behaved about Garun?"

Keril's smile grew broader. "Oh, no, no. He's been hoping you would come visit so that he might explain matters to you. Right this way, if you please." Keril guided her to Dyonis's study, even though Nia knew the way as well as she knew her own home.

When she entered, Dyonis was standing at a huge window, his back to her, overlooking a tidal-pool garden of bright anemones, sea cucumber, and coral. It was a display of wealth to have such a garden, for in order to re-create the conditions of the shallows, one had to supply more light and less pressure, and this was costly. The window itself was cut and polished from one piece of crystal, also very costly.

"Master," said Keril, "Lady Niniane is here to see you." And then he turned and swam away, leaving them alone.

"Good evening, Grandfather," Nia said.

Dyonis turned around then, and Nia could see the weariness in his eyes. He looked even older than he had the last time she had seen him. He smiled, but joy did not fill his eyes. "Ah, Nia. I'm so glad you finally came to see me." He swam over to her and gently hugged her.

"Is everything all right?"

"Yes, and no. But isn't that always the way of things?" He held out an arm to indicate the garden beyond the window. "We see the beauty of the colorful array, without thinking of the struggles of nature that cause such colors to be."

Nia scrunched up her face. "You sound very philosophical tonight," she said.

"It's a time for reexamining one's philosophy," he commented. "Now, you're here, I assume, because you wish to know why Garun was chosen over you. Am I correct?"

"Well, yes, if it isn't too rude to ask," Nia said.

"You may ask me anything; Nia, you know that," he responded.

Truly? Nia wondered. *I may put that statement to the test.* "So," she prompted, "why was I not chosen?"

Dyonis smiled gently and grasped her shoulders.

"Please understand. Were circumstances different, you would have been my first choice, and the other elders would have agreed "

"Circumstances?"

Dyonis sighed. "Now and then, it will become apparent to the High Council that a particular sort of Avatar is needed, for the sake of balance or because of a particular quality. The Councils will encourage the elders of each clan to look for candidates who have the needed quality or personality. Not every clan will choose to follow the Council's recommendation, of course—"

"But those who do have a better chance of seeing their candidate Ascend," Nia cut in flatly.

Dyonis blinked. "Oh, dear, what you must think of me. No, no, that is not the reason. I am—was—an Avatar, and I have served on the Low Council most of my life. I know how vital it is to have minds that can work together, with traits and talents complementary to one another. Therefore, alas for you, when the Councils made such a recommendation to the Bluefin Clan, I was more willing to listen than other elders." Dyonis took her hands in his. "The quality they seek, Garun has."

"And I do not."

Dyonis paused. "Correct," he said.

"What? What don't I have?"

A sad, ironic smile played on Dyonis' lips. "I can't tell you. I'm sorry, but there are things the Councils choose not to reveal about their decisions."

Nia threw out her hands in exasperation. "Well, if they've found the candidate with the personality they want, why bother with the Trials at all? Why not just declare Garun the new Avatar and be done with it?"

Dyonis shook his head. "Garun must still prove himself. He may have weaknesses we have not perceived that may become apparent during the Trials. And there may be some obscure candidate from some other clan whom the Councils had not noticed, who may prove him- or herself even better qualified. If anything, the Trials may be more necessary than ever in this instance."

"I see." Nia crossed her arms over her chest and stared at the floor. "I had been hoping for so long to become an Avatar like you, and now, because I lack some particular quality that I had no way of knowing would be needed, that chance is gone."

"I know it must seem terribly unfair, Nia. But Fortune is all too often unfair. Try as we might to force justice upon the world, Fate confounds our efforts. Please believe me when I tell you that it is all for the best."

"How can I believe you when you can't even tell me why?" Nia burst out, her voice rising. "Lately it seems this perfect home, this perfect world of Atlantis is filled with . . . half-lies and secrets."

Dyonis stared at her with raised brows. "Ah. You have come to the end of illusion," he said. "That is a difficult time of life. But nations have secrets for the same reason families have secrets, Nia. To protect those in their care."

Aha, Nia thought. *He admits our family has secrets.*

"Believe me," Dyonis went on, "despite what you may think, the government of Atlantis is outstandingly benign, particularly when you compare it to the governments of land-dweller kingdoms. We have dwelled in peace for centuries here beneath the waves, while above us kingdoms rise and fall like the tides of the sea. So tell me, Nia. What other secrets have you uncovered that have led to this new way of looking at your world?"

Now I can ask him . . . but how do I ask without getting Cephan in trouble? "Well, while talking to me after his political history lecture today, Master Zale at the Academy let something slip . . . that maybe he shouldn't have," Nia began, figuring it was the safest way to bring up the topic. "About how not every Avatar has resigned voluntarily." Nia realized that she could now be getting Master Zale in trouble, and as unpleasant as the instructor was, he surely did not deserve *that*. But it was too late now.

"Ah," said Dyonis softly. "Ma'el. He was probably referring to Ma'el."

Nia's heart raced. "Yes, um, I think that was it. Who was Ma'el?"

Dyonis sighed a heavy sigh. "I shouldn't speak of him either. But I have already kept so much hidden from you. And perhaps Ma'el's example may help you see your current situation a little more clearly. But this story must be repeated to no one, do you understand?"

"Yes, of course." Nia nodded.

Dyonis paused a moment before beginning. "Ma'el was as you are when he Ascended to the Low Council. He was intelligent, curious, strong, determined. He was training to be a physician when he joined us, and his skills in healing were phenomenal. He was already known, in the Academy, for his work in dissecting fishes and studying their inner workings. Very often, the subjects of his studies survived to swim again, thanks to his deft hands and quick mind.

"He was in the top two in nearly all of his Trials, except for the Fifth—the one of wisdom. This should have been a warning, but we paid little attention. Every one of us in the

Low Council thought him admirable and were glad to have him joined to Joab, his Farworlder king, and serve beside us. His knowledge of healing was a great asset when the Councils were called upon to use their powers, and he seemed always willing to learn from the rest of us.

"It was not until he had served with us several years that we became aware of his . . . unusual philosophy. Somehow, Ma'el felt more keenly than most Atlanteans that we had been ill served by history. He felt the Sinking had been a mistake, that it had been a cowardly act to run away from the barbaric land-dwellers. He felt that Atlantis should resurface and that we of the Council should use our powers to conquer the land-dwellers and impose our civilization upon them by force.

"Ordinarily, an Avatar's king will mitigate such strong judgmental emotions. But unbeknownst to us, Joab was strangely attuned to Ma'el's beliefs. They began to spend more time in secretive seclusion from the rest of the Councils. It was reported he was using his skills to . . . enhance the abilities of our open-sea spies. The number of ships sinking near Atlantis began to increase and we discovered that Ma'el and Joab were using their telekinetic powers for evil purposes. Obviously, we could not allow an Avatar and king with a philosophy so at odds with the peaceful charter of Atlantis to continue to serve on the Councils. I was the one to first recommend Ma'el's removal. I think he never forgave me for that."

"Oh," Nia said, not sure what else to say. *Is that why Ma'el found me so "interesting"?*

"So Ma'el and Joab were removed and punished," Dyonis went on, "and part of the sentence was that we do not speak of them."

"Why . . . I mean, what was their punishment?" Nia asked, though she knew perfectly well. "Were they banished?"

Dyonis chuckled sadly. "And unleash an Avatar and king at full power among the unsuspecting land-dwellers? We feared what he and Joab might do, so we could not banish them. But we do not execute mermyds. Therefore, they continue to live and work in Atlantis. But I will not tell you where, for that would be a grave crime, and even I would suffer for it."

"A grave crime," Nia repeated, feeling fear creep coldly around her heart. *What if I've endangered Cephan already?*

She glanced around the dark study and saw light from the tropical garden glimmering off a long, narrow object hanging on the wall. Nia swam over to it.

It's a sword, she realized once she was closer. A land-dweller weapon. She'd heard of such things in the Academy and seen them carried by guards on ceremonial occasions. Apparently they were effective in air, but in water they were nearly useless. She'd never noticed this in her grandfather's study before. "Why do you have this here, Grandfather?" she asked. "I've never seen it before."

"Ah, well, now, that has an interesting story," Dyonis said, sounding more like his old self. "It was made long, long ago, before the Sinking. Legend says it was forged by an Avatar, working with a land-dweller blacksmith. It is said that the Avatar's Farworlder king died just as the sword was being finished. As the Avatar was not long for this world himself, as a final act of friendship, he removed the oculus gland from the dead Farworlder and placed it into the hilt of that sword. It has been said ever since that the sword thereby retained some magical power of the Farworlder, particularly toward encouraging peace and friendship.

"It had been intended that the sword be given as a gift to the first land-dwelling king that the ancient Councils deemed worthy as a peace-bringer. But then the Sinking occurred, and there was no longer any chance to use the sword for that purpose. Now the sword is carried on ceremonial occasions as a symbol of the hope for peace. I brought it out for display since it will be . . . well, since it might be needed in the Ascension, if our clan is elevating one of our own."

Again, a strange comment about Garun, Nia thought. And this time from her grandfather. But right now, her attention was held by the sword. "A weapon as a symbol of peace?" she asked.

"Ironic, isn't it?" Dyonis said, winking.

"What is this inscription on the blade?" Nia asked, running her fingers over it lightly.

"It was put there by the human maker. It is in an ancient land-dweller language. I believe it reads 'Eikis Kalli Werr,' which translates roughly as 'May you possess the peace of the Great Waters.' Ah, you are about to be treated to a great honor. Someone has joined us."

Nia felt a presence behind her, and she turned around. And froze. There was Ar'an, Dyonis's Farworlder and former king, hovering just an arm's length away from her. The creature was longer than she was tall, its bulbous head alone longer than her torso. Its eyes were a reddish-gold, and its skin was brown with olive-green blotches. It reached out with one tentacle and lightly touched her hand.

Nia's heart pounded, and it was all she could do not to flinch from the Farworlder's touch. It had been one thing to face Joab separated by a wall. But it was even more unsettling to be so close that a Farworlder could touch her. She could not forget that it was an alien creature with a mind infinitely wiser than hers. She could not forget that those tentacles undulating gently on the water current could surround and crush her in an instant. She couldn't help wondering at this moment if she really *would* have been able to get past her fears if she'd been made an Avatar. Nia swallowed hard and stammered, "It . . . it . . . is an honor, M-Majesty."

A strange feeling washed over her, as if her mind were being bathed in freshened water, her thoughts soothed, her fears pushed aside. And then Nia realized it was Ar'an reaching into her mind, just as Joab had. *Oh, no! Even Ar'an is doing it! How much can Ar'an read my thoughts? Can he tell that I was lying?* Nia, unable to help herself, became even more agitated than before.

"Nia?" Dyonis asked, concerned. "What's the matter? There's no reason to be scared. Believe me, Ar'an would rather die than hurt you. You are perfectly safe."

"I—I know. I just . . . I should be leaving. My parents are expecting me. I—I have to go now. Thank you, Dyonis. Thank you, Ar'an. I have to go." Nia bowed to them both and swam as fast as she dared out of the study and out of the north window.

Is Fate trying to entrap me? she wondered frantically as she swam down to her home. *Will every Farworlder I am ever near now help itself to my thoughts? Have I just doomed Cephan and myself? What am I going to do?*

Nia slipped into her sleep chamber window and carefully replaced the netting over it. Fortunately, Tyra and Pontus had not come home yet. Nia curled up tightly in her hammock and tried to think.

Chapter Seven

"Are you sure this is allowed?" Nia asked. She looked up at the huge statue of one of the founding Avatars of Atlantis, Poseidonis, who straddled the great archway. He seemed to be staring down at her in grave disapproval.

"No, it's not allowed," Callimar replied. "That's why we're doing it."

It was the day after Nia's disturbing visit to Dyonis, and when Callimar and a few of her friends had stopped by to invite her out for an adventure, Nia had been happy for a chance to be distracted. But sneaking into the Great Arena while the competitors for the Trials were doing their training didn't seem like the best idea. Nia had done enough forbidden things recently, and adding more to the list was clearly tempting Fate.

It was also going to be painful to watch the other mermyds training. Nia still wished so much that she could be among them, getting ready for the Trials. On the other hand, it *was* a chance to possibly see Cephan—at least from a distance. That thought had finally made her decide that the trip was worth it.

Callimar was flirting like crazy, doing her best to distract the Orca guard at Poseidonis's feet. Callimar's friends—Thalassa, another Sunfish, and Pelagia, of the Mantaray Clan—took Nia by the arms and led her toward a secret entrance they knew about.

The Great Arena had been constantly rebuilt and enlarged as the population of Atlantis had grown over the centuries. Rumor had it that land-dweller architects had been consulted long ago, Farworlders not caring much for buildings. The Great Arena looked impressive and seamless from the outside, but in truth was a hodgepodge of buildings and styles, one on top of another. This meant there were occasional gaps and unintentional tunnels, as well as stairs or doorways that led nowhere. Crime was not a real issue in Atlantis, and the builders had had no reason to see that every possible entry was sealed. So a reasonably clever and curious young mermyd could always find a way in.

Nia, Thalassa, and Pelagia swam through a pillared archway onto a curved outer corridor that went around the entire arena. The three mermyds only followed it a quarter-way around, however, until they came to an ancient rope fence that was hung across a small access tunnel. The rope, though very thick, had rotted away in one place. The three of them could easily slip in, one at a time.

The access tunnel sloped up for a while, letting out at the second level of stands overlooking the ovoid arena. The original Great Arena had been designed before the Sinking, with land-dweller spectators in mind; thus the flat risers in the style of the ancient mouthbreathers. The only accommodation for mermyds had been the addition of rope loops along the stands. Mermyds could slip these over their laps to keep themselves in place. Experience over the centuries had shown that hundreds of mermyds cheering and waving easily kept the water moving well enough to keep everyone happy.

But the stands were empty at the moment, and Nia felt very conspicuous, being way up high above the central field. Far below, at the other end of the ovoid, she could see dozens of mermyds were in the midst of exercise of one form or another. She could not make out the one she had come to see, however.

The others weren't nervous at all. "This way, Nia! Hurry. Let's see how close we can get before they kick us out!"

"If we're careful enough," Nia argued, "we might not get kicked out at all. Follow me." She kicked off from one of the rows of risers and swam as fast as she could down the slope of the stands toward the field. She smiled as she heard the protests from Thalassa and Pelagia behind her.

There was a curved stone barrier wall that separated the field from the stands. Nia got right beside it, swimming low so she could not be seen from the field. She swam halfway around the arena, then stopped as she heard the voices of some of the contenders. Her heart leaped, as one of them was unmistakably Cephan's. Nia peeked over the top of the barrier.

There he was, handsome and muscular as ever, balancing a large square stone on his shoulders. *So he's practicing for the Second Trial*, Nia thought. *That's one of the most difficult. Good for him.* He glanced her way, and Nia ducked back down behind the barrier.

"Oh, so *that's* what's been on your mind," said Thalassa behind her. "Callimar mentioned you had your net out for a handsome catch."

"Maybe," Nia said with a careless shrug. To distract them from her obvious interest, she added, "But not the only thing. My mother wants to put me in Garun's job. At the Archives."

"Oooh," chorused both Thalassa and Pelagia.

"Promotional death," whispered Pelagia.

Nia nodded. "If I go there, no one will remember I even exist."

"Oh, we'll remember you," said Thalassa. "What was your name again?"

"Stop," Nia said. "I'm serious. I have to figure out some way to get out of it without making my parents furious. My father thinks it's somehow important that a Bluefin hold that post. I guess they think it should be sufficient compensation for my not being chosen for the Trials."

"It sounds like punishment to me," said Pelagia.

"It does to me too," Nia said. "But I don't know how to convince them."

"You won't," Thalassa warned. "Once elders get a thought in their heads, it becomes law. If you try to fight it, they'll just think you're being stubborn. My advice? Take the job, but do just badly enough in it to make them sorry they put you there."

"I don't think I could do that," Nia said, frowning. "If I'm put in a post, I want to do it well."

"Elders," Pelagia sighed. "They act so strange—oh, Callimar," she interrupted herself as Callimar swam up beside them. "You're finally done? You must have had a *fascinating* conversation with the Orca at the gate."

"Ha," Callimar replied, swishing her tail back and forth. "The fool just wouldn't understand that I was trying to say good-bye, so I had to keep explaining it to him. Orcas are so stupid."

"But well muscled, no?" asked Pelagia with a grin.

"Well, you can't possibly be gossiping about me," said someone swimming behind and above Nia. "I thought I heard your voice, cousin."

Nia winced. "Oh. Hello, Garun," she said without much enthusiasm.

"Hello, Garun," chorused Callimar, Thalassa, and Pelagia.

"How is your training going?" Nia asked, to be polite.

"Oh, better in some ways, worse in others."

Suddenly a figure in a black-and-white tunic loomed over them. "Who are you talking to? No visitors are permitted in the arena during the training, only participants!"

"Oh," Garun said, "this is my cousin Nia. She will be a participant—she's to be my teammate in the Third Trial. As for these others, they are here to give us advice on the course the Trial will take and what things the Council is likely to ask for."

"I see," the officious Orca replied. He frowned. "Well, finish your discussion quickly. Your talking might disturb the other trainees."

"Certainly, sir," said Garun with a nod.

As the Orca left, Nia looked at Garun with unexpected admiration. "That was fast thinking, Garun. Thanks."

Garun lifted one shoulder in a half shrug. "It was at least half true," he said. "I *have* chosen you to be my teammate in the Third Trial."

Nia's jaw dropped open. The Third Trial was a race through Atlantis to find certain objects in the city. It was swum in teams of two. The official contestant got to choose who his or her partner would be. She'd assumed that since Garun disliked her, he would choose someone else to swim with him in the Third Trial. Particularly after she had behaved so badly at his choosing ceremony. "You . . . you have?"

"Hey, Nia," Thalassa said. "You get to be in the Trials after all!"

Nia didn't know whether she should hug Garun, choke Garun, or sink into the sand floor like a halibut and cover herself over. Part of her wanted to agree right away—at least it would be a chance to participate in the Trials. Given how she expected Garun would do, it meant she could help give him a chance to succeed, help bring some glory to the name of her family.

But how could she help Cephan's competition? She knew how much being an Avatar had meant to her, and she'd seen how excited Cephan was to have the opportunity. In fact, the only reason she was happy to not have been chosen was knowing that she *wouldn't* be competing against Cephan.

"Well?" Garun asked when she didn't say anything. "You could at least say thank you."

It's wrong to deny my family a victory for my own personal reasons, she thought. Besides, even if she helped Garun win this one trial, Cephan would be able to beat him in the rest quite easily, she was sure.

"Yes, thank you, Garun," she responded with a sigh. "I'll be your second."

"Good," Garun said with a satisfied nod. "The teams will be meeting at the Marketplace at midday. Try to get some sleep the night before, won't you? I don't want to have to pull you along. Good afternoon, ladies." Garun turned tail and swam off. Nia was very tempted to stick out her tongue at his back.

"Well, there you are," said Thalassa. "They can't make you work in the Archives if you're going to be training."

"But there's no training required for the Third Trial," Nia said.

"Sure there is," said Pelagia. "You still have to swim fast and practice figuring out puzzles."

"It gives you a chance to delay, at least," Thalassa put in.

"Wait, you're going to work in the Archives?" Callimar asked.

"If my parents have anything to say about it, yes," Nia confirmed.

Callimar's eyes widened. "I hear they have a dry room in the Archives. Do you think you can handle that?"

"I'm sure I could manage," Nia said.

A dry room was a frightening place to a mermyd. A room with no water at all, only air to breathe. They had many uses—preserving paper documents; breathing bays for dolphins; places to manufacture materials, such as glass, which were difficult to make underwater. Every mermyd got the chance to go into one at least once in his or her life. In the Early Academy, mermyd children would be forced to spend some minutes in one, to show them what the land-dwelling experience of their ancestors was like. All mermyd children hated it, finding it difficult to breathe with mouth and lungs instead of gills. They hated feeling stuck to the floor, and feeling one's skin contract and itch as it dried. The experience was unpleasant enough that most mermyds vowed never to set foot or fin in a dry room again.

But Nia had adjusted the best of her school, quickly

figuring out how to breathe and stand and walk. This had only added to her "mouthbreather" reputation, and she did not remember it with pride. Only now did it occur to her that such skills might actually prove useful.

Horror stories, of course, abounded concerning dry rooms. It was said there were secret rooms throughout Atlantis where savage land-dwellers lived, ready to kill and eat the unwary mermyd who entered. It was said that any mermyd who stayed too long in a dry room would drown in all that air and die. Nia knew these stories for the foolishness they were, but she realized that here was a chance to make some points with her friends.

"That's the one part of working in the Archives I'd look forward to, actually," Nia said. "I'd enjoy the challenge. Not everybody is strong enough for a dry room, of course. But I was pretty good at getting around in one in school. I'd probably do better than Garun at that."

Sure enough, they were all staring at her with huge eyes. "Nia, you are either the bravest mermyd I have ever met, or insane," Callimar said.

"Maybe a little of both," Nia replied with a smug grin.

Suddenly the Orca official loomed over them again, with an even bigger scowl on his face and Garun in tow.

"You really have to leave now," Garun said. "I don't

want to be thrown out of the Trials just because you decided to stay and gossip."

"I was just going," Nia said.

"So were we," Callimar added. "Thank you for being so patient with us." She blinked her eyes lazily and smiled at the Orca.

His scowl turned into a sloppy grin. "Happy to help, ladies. Have a good afternoon."

Rather than reveal their knowledge of the secret entrance, they all headed blithely toward the front gate. Nia let Callimar, Thalassa, and Pelagia swim ahead, as she wondered whether she was truly as brave as her words. *And Garun is braver than I thought, given that he's had to work sometimes in a dry room all this time. Is that the quality that Dyonis was talking about, the one that Garun has and I do not?*

Something itched within her mind. It was not like the touch of Ar'an, or Joab, or even the infant Farworlder. *But . . . something . . .*

Suddenly she was grabbed from behind. Nia shrieked and struggled for a moment, until she saw it was Cephan. "Oh! It's you!" she blurted out in a mixture of relief and excitement. The trip had been worth it after all. She felt a familiar blue rush rise to her cheeks.

"Sorry," he said, letting go of her. "Just had to say hello, since you took all the trouble to come here."

"Oh. Well. I had to come to talk to Garun," she explained. She paused, wincing before continuing. "I'm going to be his teammate in the Third Trial," she admitted, hoping Cephan wouldn't be too upset.

"Congratulations!" he said with a wide smile. Nia grinned in return. How could she have been worried? Cephan was amazing—he could be happy for her, even knowing that she had agreed to compete against him. "Now I'm going to have to pick my second carefully," he went on, his eyes sparkling. "You'll be a tough team to beat. Frankly, if they'd let us choose across clans, I'd have picked you myself." He glanced around. "I've gotta run. I'm not supposed to socialize during training time." He gave her a long, intense look, and Nia felt a chill go through her—but a *good* kind this time, unlike what she'd felt when she met Ma'el. "I'll see you soon," he said softly; then he swam away back toward the field.

Nia laughed, suddenly giddy. Cephan always had that effect on her. Then she realized the mental itch she'd felt earlier was gone. She'd probably just imagined it, anyway, she told herself as she turned and swam for home.

Chapter Eight

The next two days were almost normal for Nia. She informed her parents that she couldn't possibly alter her schedule now, since she had to use her extra time to privately train for the Third Trial. Her parents were very understanding, of course, since she would be helping Garun win. And it seemed they thought that was the most important thing in the world.

So she did her early-day duties at the Farworlder nursery, noting that the little ones were still crankier than usual. They wouldn't even calm down when she sang to them, which had worked in the past, or when she gave them Cephan's glass ball to play with. She was beginning to wonder whether it was a stage in their development. If so, perhaps escaping to a future, at least temporarily, in the Archives would not be such a bad thing. In the afternoons, she would work on puzzles and practice riddles and swim laps around the Dome. For a time, she tried not to worry too much about meddling Farworlder minds, or what mysterious quality she lacked, or the Archives position, or when she would see Cephan again, or her parents' strange and secretive obsessions.

The first day of the Trials for Ascension came all too soon. After doing an afternoon lap through the city, swimming as fast as she dared, Nia found herself caught up in the crowd of mermyds heading along the broad main avenue toward the Great Arena. She allowed herself to follow the flow with them, enjoying how the water bubbled and hummed with their excited babble. The enthusiasm around her was contagious—the Trials were events no one in Atlantis wanted to miss. Even though tonight was only the Opening Ceremonies, everyone seemed to be caught up in the festive spirit.

But Nia, drifting in the slipstream of the mermyds swimming ahead of her, couldn't help feeling a trace of anxiety as well as excitement. She was going to have to be gracious, and supportive of Garun's efforts, and pleasant to her family, with whom she was going to be stuck in an observation box for a few hours. It promised to be a very trying evening. Even the chance to get another glimpse of Cephan might not quite make up for it.

This time she entered the arena through the great arch, along with everyone else, between the legs of Poseidonis.

Nia wondered how many mermyds knew about the secret entrances to the arena. Given how many children she saw peeling away from the crowd to scurry around the sides of the building, she gathered there were quite a few.

The Great Arena was a much more impressive sight this evening than it had been just days before. It was ablaze with glowing puffer-fish lanterns, and the stands were filled with colorfully dressed mermyds. A current of freshened water swept around the outer curve of the arena—apparently one of the cross-city currents had been redirected for the event. Scores of Orca guards had been positioned to keep the spectators from swimming out over the field, and were guiding them to their seats. Now and then a mischievous mermyd child would zip past one of the guards and do somersaults and barrel-rolls over the field. This would lead to a lively chase, providing some preshow entertainment.

Nia kicked herself away from the crowd at the entrance and swam off in search of the Bluefin observation box. It would be close to the edge of the competition field itself. The Bluefin Clan, with its Council connections, was entitled to such luxury.

Nia thought she spotted a banner with her family's colors, blue and silver, at the far end of the arena. She found the side entrance to the Bluefin observation box, and Sala, wearing the frilly pink colors of the Shrimp Clan, opened the door for her. Nia swam in.

Her parents, Dyonis, and her uncle Skiff and aunt Maru, Garun's parents, were huddled in close discussion as Nia entered. Dyonis's white hair drifted around his face, and the wide sleeves of his blue-and-silver ceremonial jacket billowed around him. He was bending toward the others and saying softly, "Now, during the second hour I will be in deep concentration, so—ah, Nia!" He looked up at her, but his smile seemed forced. "So glad you could join us."

"Um, hello," Nia said, feeling a little awkward. The water in the box had gotten suddenly, distinctly chilly. The relatives had clearly not expected her to come in on their discussion.

"Nia, dear," Aunt Maru said in greeting as she swam up to Nia, her yellow-green eyes wide in her small, narrow face. Taking Nia's hands in hers, Maru said, "I wanted to thank you ever so much for agreeing to be Garun's teammate in the Third Trial. I know you must have been disappointed not to be chosen, but I hope this in some small way makes up for that." There was tension in her face—sorrow, desperation, fear flickering in her eyes.

Nia wondered what could possibly be going on. Perhaps they were all still guilty over Nia not having been chosen.

"Um, thank you. I mean, you're welcome. I just want to do the right thing for the honor of my clan," Nia said. "I'm sure Garun was chosen for good reasons, and I will do my best to support him."

"That's the spirit!" said Aunt Maru, patting Nia's hand.

"So glad you could make it, Nia, dear!" exclaimed Tyra, though something in her tortoise-shell-colored brown eyes showed that her feelings were mixed. Her glossy dark-green hair, the color of kelp, was done up with elaborate combs of mother-of-pearl. Strands of pearls hung down from her waist, and she had had her tail scales polished until they were almost blinding. As always, Nia was struck with how different she looked from her mother; how her light, silvery blond hair contrasted with her mother's deep-green shade. There was little resemblance between them in any of their features, in fact, and Nia sometimes wondered if this was why her mother never seemed completely comfortable with her. Perhaps she was always disappointed that her only child looked —and acted—nothing like her.

"You look . . . dazzling, Mother," Nia said, meaning it.

The Trials were the sort of event where the high-born went to see and be seen—there was more competition going on than just that on the field.

"Isn't she sweet?" Tyra crooned. "Have you had anything to eat, Nia? You're looking so thin these days. Here." Her mother handed Nia a cone of seaweed filled with shredded crab and bits of raw tuna, held together with anchovy paste.

"I've been training, Mother," Nia explained. "Fat makes you float and slows you down." But training also makes an athlete hungry, and Nia suddenly felt ravenous. She devoured the nori-cone in five bites. It tasted savory and salty. At least the Bluefins always hired good cooks.

"That's better. Athletes need to get their energy from somewhere," Tyra lectured.

"You know, I was thinking the other day," Nia said, "that it might be wonderful to have baleen, like whales do, instead of teeth in the mouth? Then swimmers could just go and go and go, sucking up food from the water as they went. The faster you went, the more food you'd gather. The more food you'd gather, the faster and longer you could swim. You'd never have to stop for meals."

"What an . . . interesting notion," Tyra said, bewildered.

Across the room, Dyonis was regarding her with a

smile that was half amused, half disturbed. Nia decided she ought to say *something* to him, after her awkward, hasty departure from his study days before. "I am glad to see you, Grandfather. But you didn't bring Ar'an with you. Doesn't he like to watch the Opening Ceremonies?"

The strange expression this brought to Dyonis's face was unreadable. "Ar'an will be watching with others of his kind. Shall I pass along to him your . . . greeting?"

"If you could also pass along an apology," Nia said.

"There is no need," Dyonis reassured her. "Although I could arrange for you to apologize to him in person, if you wish."

"No! No, thanks. I . . . wouldn't want to trouble him." Nia decided it was time to keep her mouth shut.

"The Ceremonies are about to begin," her mother said. "Come. Sit." Tyra guided Nia toward the front of the box. There, in some mouthbreather's idea of comfort, were chairs made of giant padded clam shells. Nia curled up on one but declined to use the seat strap.

She heard a soft *floomp* and saw her father settling his wide girth into the other clamshell chair beside her. He began speaking to no one in particular. "Ah, these are great days for us, great days. Wouldn't miss this for all the coral in the sea."

As usual, Nia didn't quite know what to say to him. "My training's been going well, Father. This afternoon I did a circuit of the city in my fastest time yet, without even using the flow-currents."

"Hmm, well that's good. That's good." Pontus tilted his head back and closed his eyes.

"I ate a sea slug just to see what it tasted like."

"Hmm, yes, that's good, that's . . . eh, *what?*" He finally looked at her.

"Just checking," Nia said with a teasing grin.

Pontus shook his head. "You are a strange child." He closed his eyes again.

Definitely time to keep my mouth shut, Nia thought with a sigh. She could taste on the water that her father had been drinking a good bit of the seaweed wine already. Still, his words were painful to her.

Nia gazed out toward the field, hoping to catch a glimpse of Cephan. There were some dark-haired young mermyds at the far end of the field, but she couldn't be sure one of them was him.

"Trying to see a bit closer, are you?" Dyonis asked her. "Here, use this. It's an invention of the Farworlders." He extended a tube out of the wall below the arch in front of them and a picture immediately appeared on the wall.

"Just look through the tube and point it at what you want to see. You'll see a close picture of it there on the wall. The longer you extend the tube, the closer you can look. Pretty amazing, isn't it? Give it a try."

Carefully holding the tube in one hand, Nia pointed it toward the group of dark-haired young men. Turning to the picture on the wall, she could see one of them was, indeed, Cephan. He was looking very handsome, wearing bands of cloth across his chest in the dark sand and gray of his clan.

Her mother swam over and gently grasped her wrist. "If you're looking to set your net for a worthwhile catch, *here's* where you should place your regard." Tyra moved Nia's arm until the tube was pointed toward a cluster of young men closer to the box. These were wearing the gold and yellow-green of the Sunfish Clan. They were handsome enough, but Nia knew them to be rude, arrogant fellows. And after some of the things Callimar had told her about their snobbish behavior, Nia found it impossible to be interested in them.

"It is among *those* you will find a fulfilling mate someday," Tyra said.

Nia worked very hard at not laughing. *Wonderful. First my mother wants to meddle in my career, and now she wants to meddle in my love life too.*

Suddenly the water around them vibrated with the eerie drone of a hundred conchshell trumpets being played. The competitors above the field all swam over to the side walls.

"Aha!" her father cried, sitting up. "The Opening Ceremonies begin! Let's hope they're not as dull as they were the last time."

Nia had not been alive the last time an Avatar was chosen, so she had no idea what her father meant.

Music began, and a huge school of trained squid wriggled into the arena, hovering over the center of the field. Their phosphorescence pulsed pink, blue, and green, in time with the music.

"Oh, no," Pontus moaned. "They're doing the History of the Farworlders again."

"Hush, dear," Tyra said. "It's tradition."

The squid swirled into various formations, each more dazzling than the last. One set seemed to depict a great, glimmering city. Another seemed to show a battle, with two groups of squid fighting each other. As the final formation, the squids organized into a glowing sun, the shape of the royal symbol, and then swam bursting outward, as if the sun had exploded, hundreds of shimmering shards of life spreading out through the dark waters.

Nia watched, fascinated, trying to remember her Farworlder history. She knew they had come from another ocean far away, but it had been difficult for her to grasp the idea of an even vaster ocean, an ocean of darkness without water or even air, that lay between the worlds.

The trained squid built another formation, which Nia recognized. It was Atlantis before the Sinking, a sparkling pyramid shining in sunlight. *How could any mermyds, let alone land-dwellers, not be blinded by such a sight?* Nia wondered.

Then the squid with blue and green phosphorescent lights wriggled up and around the city formation, covering it over. Bit by bit, bottom to top, the lights winked out, reenacting the Sinking. Pontus's neck gills stretched wide in a yawn that disturbed the water all around him.

Tyra slapped his shoulder gently. "Really, dear, try to show some courtesy."

The next display was a sinuous dance by the mermyds of the Moray Clan, for which Nia's father was curiously silent and attentive. Nia thought the male Morays weren't nearly as handsome as Cephan, but they did have a certain gracefulness. The female Morays seemed able to bend their bodies into impossible positions, and Nia admired the muscle strength they must have to make it look so effortless.

At last, with flourishes of their tails, the Morays left the performance space. With a loud pop and a *wheeeee!*, suddenly a troop of porpoises rushed over the field into the middle. Everyone in the arena cheered, for they all loved the porpoises. Usually, the dolphins and porpoises of Atlantis delivered packages and messages, found lost children, and could give you a fast ride somewhere, if you needed it.

But in the Opening Ceremonies, the porpoises got a chance to show off. They did a frenetic dance while singing a silly song that to Nia sounded like "Yakkety-yak, yakkety-yak" and a lot of clicks. It was said that the Farworlders could understand the porpoise language. *In which case, an Avatar should be able to understand them too*, Nia thought. She turned her head and looked at Dyonis. He was smiling and chuckling to himself. She felt envious. "What are they singing about, Dyonis?"

"Hmm? Oh . . . it, um . . . it doesn't translate very well," was all he would say.

The porpoises finished their song and dashed off to their dry-room breathing chambers under the arena. Unlike mermyds, porpoises could not breathe water, so they had to surface to breathe air in the special sealed rooms. Legend had it that these dry rooms had originally been made for the few surviving humans who had been trapped on

Atlantis at the Sinking. Nia remembered learning at the Academy how difficult it was to take air from the sea to fill those chambers. Even despite such aid, the stories said, the ancient land-dweller survivors had not lasted more than a few months. Tragic plays and poems had been written about those mythical land-dwellers' last days.

To spend the rest of your life locked in one room, Nia thought with a shudder. *How could anyone bear it?* She remembered Ma'el and Joab in their cell in the Lower Depths. *Whatever he did, was it worth such punishment? Wouldn't banishment have been more kind?*

Oohs and ahs burbled through the arena as an enormous, long shape appeared overhead and then descended nearly to the level of the field. It was an elderly blue whale that the city of Atlantis had adopted—she was often seen swimming just beyond the Dome. *How did they get her into the city?* Nia wondered. The whale practically filled the whole arena.

And then the whale sang, her incredibly powerful and deep voice resonating through the water, through every mermyd body. She sang without words, but Nia heard in her long tones the loneliness of the wide ocean, the beauty and serenity of the depths of the sea. She sang of eternity.

Nia was enthralled, and she felt her eyes sting with the

urge to cry, but fought it down. She noticed her mother and aunt blinking more than usual, as well. The whale finished her song and ascended again, out of the arena. The cheers of the assembled mermyds were heartfelt as they watched her go.

"Good, it's over," Pontus said. "The fat old lady has sung. Now we can get on to the real stuff."

"Pontus!" Tyra cried, scandalized.

"What? I'm here to watch Garun, not to see this foo-farah."

Nia buried her face in her hands and sank deeper into the cushion of the clamshell chair. How could anyone claim *her* behavior was embarrassing?

Another *whoooom* of the conch shells, like a herd of whales sounding in unison, announced that the Parade of Competitors was about to begin. Each contestant, one from each of the thirty-two clans, would swim around the arena, bearing the clan banner.

Nia sat up, wondering what, if anything, she should do when Cephan swam by. *Something as subtle as a wink? No, he probably wouldn't see that. Should I wave? My parents might notice that. Just smile? Should I do nothing and let him wonder why I'm being haughty?* Nia chewed on her thumb-webbing, unable to decide.

"Do you think Garun will be first?" Aunt Maru asked.

"That's impossible to say," Tyra replied. "In the name of fairness, they are supposed to pick the order of clans randomly."

"But, I mean, with all the . . ." Suddenly Aunt Maru glanced at Nia. "I mean, of course. Rank shouldn't make any difference. It would be impossible to know."

Why are they acting so strangely? Nia wondered, feeling her skin begin to creep. *Am I imagining things, or does everyone seem uncomfortable around me?* Nia huddled in her chair, knees to her chin, and tried to seem as harmless as possible, focusing her attention on the parade.

The first candidate was the entrant from the Sunfish Clan. *So much for random choice*, Nia thought. *They probably insisted on being first no matter what.* Carrying the gold-and-yellow-green banner, the mermyd swam proudly by. He was thinner than Nia liked, and he'd actually had his fin scales painted gold to match the banner. Nia thought that a bit gaudy.

Next was the contestant for the Dolphin Clan, a mermyd carrying a gray-and-white banner. At least she seemed to be having fun, smiling and waving at everybody. Nia couldn't help but wave back, even though she didn't know her.

Third came Garun. He was also smiling, waving his blue-and-silver banner back and forth. Everyone in the Bluefin booth leaped up in the water and cheered. Nia did too, since she was trying to be a good sport. *Enjoy your Trials, Garun. You'll never know how badly I wish it could be me*.

Next to go by was the Mantaray contestant in an elegant tunic of dark and light gray. Nia's parents, aunt, and uncle lost interest after that, their conversation becoming louder. Nia huddled in her chair, bored, hardly paying attention anymore.

Then there he was. Nia sat up so fast she floated off her chair as Cephan swam by. He turned on his side a moment, grinned and winked at her, and then swam on. Nia clapped her hands and nearly bobbed up and down. "He smiled at me!" she said softly. "He smiled at me!" She turned her head and saw that her parents were frowning at her.

Tyra leaned close to her. "Admire whomever you like, Nia," she whispered. "But when it comes time for you to select a permanent mate, try to be serious about your choice."

Nia crossed her arms over her chest and did not reply, worried she might say something to get herself in trouble as the anger built within her.

She endured silently through the rest of the parade. When it was finished, she tried to slip out the door.

"Where are you going, dear?" Tyra asked. "The party's just about to begin."

"I know," Nia said. "I'm going to congratulate Garun on his fine showing while I still have a chance. Once the party gets going, I expect I won't be able to get near him."

"Well, send him to us when you find him!" Uncle Skiff cried.

"Yes, Uncle. I will." Nia exchanged glances with Dyonis, but quickly glanced away when she saw the questioning look in his eyes. She decided to leave before he asked her any questions.

The whole arena would become one big party now—some claimed it was the Unnumbered Trial, since contestants were expected to participate. Those candidates who left the party to conserve their strength were thought to be slightly cheating.

Nearly the whole crowd of spectators was converging on the contestants' area, so Nia was surrounded in a crush of other mermyds. Suddenly, there it was again . . . the itching in her brain, as if a Farworlder, or something like it, was trying to touch her thoughts. Nia looked around wildly, but there were no Farworlders in this throng.

Unnerved, Nia turned aside and fought her way out of the mass of mermyds, elbowing and kicking quite a few as she went. She didn't care about the damage this might do to her already tarnished reputation. She just needed to find a quiet space to think. She found her way to an empty entrance tunnel and curled up next to the wall, holding her head.

Am I going crazy? My family is acting so strange! And why do I keep feeling this thing in my mind?

"Nia?"

She gasped and looked up. It was Cephan, peering into the tunnel. "Cephan!" She launched herself toward him, using just a little too much energy in her stroke. He caught her around the waist just as she was about to go by him.

"Hey!" he said, smiling. She couldn't help feeling a twinge of disappointment when he let go of her. It felt so perfect to have his arms around her. "Your family might see us here," he warned. "I know someplace more private." He brushed away a layer of sea moss and muck from the stone wall, revealing a door in the middle of the tunnel. He opened it and guided her in. They were in a long-unused storage space under the stands, another one of the accidental rooms created by the rebuilding of the arena. A lone discarded phosphor-globe provided the only light. With the door closed, the hubbub of the crowd seemed far away.

"How do you know about places like this?" Nia asked, gazing around her in amazement.

"We worker fellows all talk to one another. We let one another know the best places for . . . a shortcut or hiding stuff or . . . privacy." He looked down at her shyly, and Nia silently cursed the fact that she blushed so easily. "Now why were you in that tunnel all by yourself?" he asked.

Nia took a deep breath. "Promise you won't tease me or laugh at me?" she said.

"I promise."

"I've told you before, I think I can feel a Farworlder touching my mind—especially in the nursery. But lately I've been feeling something strange . . . it's like a Farworlder's mental touch, but different."

"And you felt it just now, right before you went into the tunnel?"

"Yes. And the last time I was here at the arena, just before I left."

"Wow." He smiled.

"Oh, don't tease me, please."

"I'm not teasing. I believe you. I'm . . . astonished. You realize no mermyd has ever had that kind of power unjoined before?"

"Of course I know that. That's why I don't tell anyone."

Cephan moved closer to her, so close she shivered. "This is wonderful," he said. "You're the most incredible mermyd."

Nia's face heated up, and she wondered whether Cephan would kiss her cheek again—or kiss her for real, finally!

"If only I knew who it was," she said with a sigh. "It may be incredible, but I wish it would stop. I don't know, perhaps it *is* from a Farworlder. But there can't be any Farworlders in the arena, can there?"

"Of course there are," Cephan said. "They're watching the Trials just like everyone else. They've got secret chambers all over these stands. Didn't you know?"

Nia pressed her lips together. "No. But that makes sense. Dyonis said his Farworlder was watching with others of his kind. And if the dolphins have dry rooms, of course the Farworlders can have their own special rooms."

"There you are. Maybe that's just more of the information we worker guys share. Not everyone would know that, I suppose."

Nia frowned. "It must be Ar'an, then. He reached out to me when I visited my grandfather. And . . . I was very scared. It doesn't *seem* to be a Farworlder, and it feels different from the way it did that night . . . but it must be him, right?" She sighed. None of this made sense. "But why would Ar'an do it again?" she asked, exasperated.

"Ar'an . . . a former king . . . wow." Cephan paused a moment, then went on, "Well, maybe your grandfather is worried for you."

"Worried for me? I don't know if that's it, exactly. My whole family was acting strange tonight. They'd start to talk about things and then stop if they saw me listening."

"They probably don't want to upset you," Cephan said. "Now that their attention is all on your cousin, they must be afraid that overhearing them talk about Garun will just hurt you."

Nia nodded. It did make sense. Another question occurred to her, one she needed to ask. "Cephan, you've watched Garun train now. What do you think of him, as a competitor?"

Cephan paused. "What do I think? Well, I've mostly been concentrating on my own work. We're not supposed to watch other competitors, though everyone does. I have to say I haven't noticed anything special, one way or the other. He seems pretty smart, but he may have trouble in the races. As for the rest . . ." Cephan shrugged. "I know nothing about his wisdom or magical ability."

Nia sighed. "Well, it was worth a try. My family all seem worried that he's not going to do well, and yet they're desperate to see him win."

"That sounds like what you'd expect, doesn't it? All the competitors I've talked to say their families are acting a little strangely. Although . . . there is some grumbling on the field about the extra coaching Garun's been getting. Rumors that he's getting too much help to be strictly . . ." Cephan trailed off, avoiding Nia's gaze.

"What?" she pressed. "What are you trying to say?"

"I shouldn't be passing along rumors," Cephan mumbled. "That isn't fair, and they'd only upset you. I'd better go. I have to join the party or there will be questions asked. Just . . . take it easy on yourself, all right? Be careful." He gave her a small smile. "I'll talk to you again when I can." He escorted her out of the little room and then swam away.

Somehow I don't think this is a time for taking it easy, Nia thought. *I've got to start finding out the truth before I explode.*

Chapter Nine

It was a holiday in Atlantis, and everyone whose energy had survived the parties of the night before (and even those whose hadn't) were coming back to the Great Arena to witness the exciting First and Second Trials. Even Nia.

But her enthusiasm had been replaced by determination and a more calculating perspective. Now, when she swam under the great arch of Poseidonis and out among the stands, she wondered where the secret chambers of the Farworlder kings were hidden. How near might she be to any of them? She wondered where Garun was being trained and whether there was a way she might sneak in for a look. When she swam into the Bluefin observation box, she noted the cool greetings her parents and aunt and uncle gave her. When she saw Dyonis, it took effort to smile.

Dyonis pulled her aside as soon as he noticed her. "You know, Nia, you do not need to stay if you are finding these events . . . uncomfortable. I know how much you'd rather be participating than watching. If you decided to not be present, except for the Third Trial, of course, I'm sure everyone would understand."

And now he's treating me like a child, Nia thought sourly, *though he never has before*. "No," Nia said firmly and, she hoped, respectfully. "I want to stay. I want to show that I can be relied upon. To give the support and enthusiasm properly due Garun as the chosen of my clan. To do otherwise would be immature and cowardly."

Dyonis sighed. "It is not cowardly to admit to one's feelings, Nia. But, very well. How can anyone deny such a noble intention?" He gestured grandly to one of the clamshell chairs, and Nia swam over and settled in.

"Besides," Nia announced, not caring who was listening, "I'm still an athlete, and these are the most exciting Trials to watch for someone with my training. I expect to enjoy myself no matter who wins."

Pontus was again in the chair beside her, head tilted back, fast asleep. Nia could tell from the water around him that he'd been sucking down the seaweed wine again.

Tyra swam over. "You'll have to forgive Pontus, dear. He had a very late night of it. We haven't seen a party like that in years. By the way, where were you?"

"I went home early," Nia said, which was what she'd

done after saying good-bye to Cephan. "I had a lot to think about."

"Oh." Nia could hear the curiosity in her mother's voice, but she said nothing more. "Would you like some refreshment?" Tyra asked when the pause had gotten a little too long. "The food hasn't arrived yet, but we have some kelp juice."

"That would be fine, thank you," Nia said.

Tyra handed Nia a bladder gourd. The gourds were grown on a special breed of kelp in the farms Down Below. They had strawlike appendages that you bit off in order to suck the juice out. The only problem was that you either had to drink it all at once, or carefully pinch the straw between sips. Otherwise, seawater got in with the juice, ruining the taste.

Nia was glad, however, to keep her mouth occupied so she wouldn't have to talk to anyone.

The arena was all set up for the First Trial. At the far end of the oval field, to the right of the Bluefin box, there was a metal rack, two mermyd heights tall, with thirty-two slots along it. Already some of the contestants were starting to place themselves in the slots along the rack. Nia thought she could see Cephan among them. She also thought she could see Garun in the middle of the rack, but she didn't want to use the farseeing tube just yet.

The First Trial was simply a race from one end of the oval arena to the other. The first swimmer to touch the golden pole at the other end was the winner. But the main thing was not to be among the last six, for those six competitors would be dismissed, no longer able to participate in the rest of the Trials.

Racers could also be disqualified if they let their feet or tail touch the arena bed. It was expected that the racers would all swim at the same level at which they started. They could swim higher, but it was poor strategy, since it would usually slow them down. Nia had often swum races like this during her physical training at the Academy. She had even won a few. She could almost feel what it would be like to swim this course, with these many competitors, what her strategy would be depending on whether she had tailed or legged swimmers beside her, or strong or weak ones. But that made her feel all the more sad that she wasn't participating.

The slots began to fill with competitors, and the noises of anticipation of the crowd grew louder. Nia noticed a peculiar taste to the water with so many excited mermyds in the same place. It made the excitement almost truly contagious.

The conchshell trumpets sounded a long, low moan, waking Pontus up with a start. "Huh, wha?"

"Shh," Tyra hissed. "It's beginning."

On a platform directly across the arena from the Bluefin booth, the senior Avatar on the Low Council, Xemos, came forward. Nia's father moved the farseeing tube so that a clear picture of Xemos appeared on the wall. Two of the Ceremonial Guard, carrying long spears and wearing armor of sea-dragon scales, appeared on either side of him.

"Fellow Atlanteans," Xemos began, and the crowd quieted. Nia wondered if he was using some form of Farworlder magic to make himself heard so well. "On behalf of the High and Low Councils, I welcome you. While we regret that our comrade Thaumas and his king, Bo'az, have left our ranks, that sorrow is now replaced with anticipation. For today begin the great Trials that will bring to us our new associate, our next Avatar. The finest youth of all our clans will be tested.

"Those who are best in strength and in wisdom will contend for the honor of being joined to a Farworlder, of having their knowledge and power expanded beyond the imagining of any mermyd. He or she who is best in all will achieve that honor and Ascend to join our ranks."

Nia frowned, wondering about the Farworlder end of things. She knew that the kings of the High Council chose which infant Farworlder would be the next king, but the manner in which it was chosen was secret. Nia knew one of her charges at the nursery was going to be joined to the next Avatar, but she did not know which one or by what criteria the creature would be chosen. She turned around in her chair and asked her grandfather, "Dyonis, how do the Farworlders choose their next king?"

Her question seemed to startle Dyonis out of some intense concentration, and for a split second he glared angrily at her. Then his face softened, and he replied, "Not now, Nia. Later, please. Watch the race." He nodded toward the field.

Nia turned back around. *Well. That was interesting*, she told herself, trying to keep the hurt at bay. Her beloved grandfather had never, ever snapped at her before.

"It is with great joy, therefore," Xemos finished, "that I open this, the First Trial toward the Ascension. Let the race begin!"

The crowd cheered, and the water almost boiled with the sound. While her father was applauding, Nia grabbed the farseeing tube and turned it toward the starting gates. Sure enough, there was Cephan, fourth from the left, Nia scanned the others in the rack. They were about evenly split between those with tails and those with two legs. Those with tails, like Cephan, had an early advantage over those with legs, like Garun, for the tail could give an enormous initial burst of speed. Mermyd tails, however, were not as well suited to endurance as legs were, and it was easier for two-legged swimmers to use their arms in coordination. The strategy for a tailed swimmer was to open up a great enough lead at the beginning that no one could catch up. The strategy for two-legged swimmers was to hope that the tailed swimmers tired quickly.

Nia's father snatched back the farseeing tube and centered the image, naturally, on Garun. Garun's pale face was set in a frown of grim determination as he gripped the poles at either side of his gate. *Please don't embarrass us, Garun*, Nia thought.

The conchshell trumpets sounded, and the starting gates opened. The racers rushed out of the rack. Sure enough, to Nia's delight, Cephan pulled out ahead of the pack of swimmers. Nia sat forward in her chair, lightly pounding her knees with her fists. "Go, Cephan," she whispered.

The two sides began pulling ahead, as Pontus had predicted. Garun was kicking and stroking for all he was worth, but it was clear he was struggling. He began to rise above the plane of the other swimmers and Nia knew then he had no chance. That was a strategy only the most powerful swimmers could use to advantage.

Nia felt a momentary headache and rubbed her forehead. *Ouch. What was in that kelp juice? It didn't taste like wine.* But she forced herself to try to ignore the pain as she looked out again at the field.

Suddenly one of the swimmers, a Moray, veered into the path of another. The Moray's fins seemed to tangle up with the other swimmer's legs in an awkward movement, and together they flopped through the water, bumping into the swimmers next to them. A cry of disbelief roared out from the crowd, followed by stunned silence as one by one swimmers were knocked, spinning, out of their lanes by a neighbor. Only Cephan, who was far enough ahead, and Garun, who was swimming above, were free from the flailing arms, slapping tails, and kicking legs of the other racers. Two of the knotted throng of competitors began fighting and, not noticing where they were, drifted down until their feet touched the arena floor, disqualifying them. Accidents in a field this crowded were not uncommon, but Nia had never seen anything like this in any race she had been in or watched. Her parents didn't seem to notice the oddness of it. "Go, Garun!" they were cheering, as if nothing strange was happening.

Cephan was apparently so intent upon his goal that he never looked back. He easily reached the golden pole first. It took Nia a few moments to let it sink in. "Cephan won? Cephan won! Cephan won!"

She stopped as she noticed her parents staring at her. "How well, exactly, do you know this Cephan?" her father asked.

"Um . . ." she began, but before she could invent a story, Dyonis came up behind Pontus and put a hand on his shoulder.

"Look," Dyonis said, "it appears these strange circumstances favor our Garun well."

Sure enough, Garun had managed to keep his pace steady enough that, even though some of the other swimmers had now disentangled themselves from the mess, they could not catch up. Garun was second to touch the golden pole.

Everyone in the Bluefin box erupted in cheers, and Nia found herself bounced around by the water's agitation. She cheered too, disbelievingly, thinking, *Well, he certainly didn't disgrace us. But that tangle the others got into was the only way he could have finished so well.* She looked at Dyonis, who was gazing out at the field with a concerned frown. The last of the swimmers were churning the water, trying not to be among the last six to touch the pole. The unfortunates who had set foot on the arena bed slowly and despondently swam off the field.

"Grandfather," Nia said to Dyonis. "So much went wrong—shouldn't this race be set aside and run again?"

Her parents looked at her as if she'd suggested eating spiny urchins. "Nia, how can you even *suggest* such a thing?" Tyra demanded. "You know how Garun must conserve his strength."

"That will be up to the High Council, Nia," Dyonis replied. "Ah, here comes Xemos again. I'm sure he'll explain."

The conchshell trumpets sounded another moan, and the Avatar Xemos again swam out onto the platform. "Citizens of Atlantis: There has been some question as to the legitimacy of this First Trial."

"No!" Pontus cried.

"They wouldn't dare!" Tyra said.

"However," Xemos went on, "the High Council has already made its ruling. This First Trial shall stand."

Tyra and Aunt Maru hugged each other and then

hugged Uncle Skiff. Pontus declined to be hugged, but he allowed himself to look smug.

"There, you see?" Pontus growled at Nia. "Disqualify the race *indeed*. How dare you call yourself a Bluefin?"

"I—I'm sorry," Nia said. "I just wondered what was fair."

Loud, continuous cheering was coming from a far section of the arena. Nia noticed many of those spectators were wearing the colors of the Stingray, Cephan's clan. *How could I have asked whether the race should be disqualified? Cephan won. What is wrong with me?*

"I regret to announce," Xemos continued, "that the disqualified clans are these: Sandcrab, Monkfish, Mako, Shad, Sea Turtle, and Otter." Moans of disappointment rolled through the water from various sections of the arena. "Please take some time," Xemos continued, "to refresh yourselves, and to give our competitors some rest. We will begin the Second Trial in an hour."

Refreshments arrived at the Bluefin box promptly. Sala had brought a special delicacy—scalded shrimp wrapped in seaweed pastry. Cooked food was rare in the mermyd diet, because it was so difficult to do underwater. Because it was rare and difficult, it was, of course, more fashionable. Nia knew these scalded shrimp had been prepared, at great risk to the cooks, in the very same steam vents Down Below that Cephan had mentioned to her. Nia bit into the pastry and found it was still slightly warm—a strange sensation. The food gave everyone a reason not to talk to Nia, for which she was grateful.

Nia went up to the front of the observation box and looked out at the arena, noticing that the ache she'd had in her head was completely gone. It had been since the end of the race. *Actually, it was only there from right before the race went wrong until Garun finished*, she realized with a start. She glanced back over her shoulder at Dyonis, who avoided her gaze. Then she recalled what Cephan had started to say the other night . . . the rumors about cheating. She'd read that Farworlder magic, when used by Farworlders or their Avatars, could cause physical pain in the mermyd Avatars whose senses were attuned.

But I'm not even an Avatar, she told herself. Still, she *did* feel the touch of Farworlders, despite being told repeatedly that it wasn't possible. Nia shook her head and chided herself. *No honorable Avatar would ever misuse his power . . . unless he was, in truth, dishonorable—like Ma'el.* Nia couldn't believe her grandfather would actually manipulate the trials to allow Garun to win. She turned her attention back to the arena field.

The high rack of starting gates was being removed from the field, to be replaced by a lower rack in preparation for the Second Trial. Workers were bringing out large square stones and piling them beside the starting gate rack.

In this Trial, each entrant would be given one of the stones to carry on the shoulders. Again, the racer had to reach the golden pole on the far side of the field. But this was a test more of endurance than speed. One could touch the arena floor if one wished—indeed, those with two legs usually preferred to walk the race rather than swim it. This gave two-legged mermyds some advantage over the tailed sort, although a mermyd with a strong tail could manage. Nia had heard once of a tailed mermyd who had won a Second Trial by bouncing down the field on his hind flipper like a hopping sea scallop. She wondered whether Cephan would try it that way.

She was jolted out of her reverie by the sounding of the conchshell trumpets and the reappearance of Xemos on the announcement platform. "Will the contestants for the Second Trial please take their places at the gates?" he declared.

The gate began to fill up with each clan representative, in a different order this time, and Nia could discern no particular pattern. She noticed that some of the clans with brighter colors were toward one side of the field; the Tang Clan with its bright oranges, the Lobster Clan in blue and red, the Sea Cucumber Clan with purple and yellow, the Anemone Clan in magenta and white. Nia had occasionally wished, when she was younger, that she had been born to one of these clans. Always having to wear blue and silver on ceremonial occasions had gotten rather dull.

Everyone in the Bluefin box pressed forward to see where Garun was, which made Nia feel hemmed in. Her father used the farseeing tube and centered Garun in its projection. Garun was in the middle again. Nia peered at the starting gate lineup and saw that Cephan was all the way at the far end.

Workers took up the stones and delivered one to each contestant, helping them settle the block on their shoulders. Most competitors were able to position the stone comfortably right away, but a few were having trouble. Garun seemed to be one of them—he nearly doubled over under the weight of his. Nia's parents and cousins shouted encouragement at his image on the wall, but, of course, he couldn't hear them.

The workers stepped back, and the conchshell trumpets sounded again. The gates opened, and the contestants staggered out. Nia could see a couple of the tailed mermyds trying the hopping strategy, but they were having difficulty with balance. One hopped too low, couldn't get his tail back under him, and was smashed to the arena bed by his stone. Cephan was doing a combination wriggle-hop that kept him higher in the water, but he was having trouble keeping the stone settled on his shoulders, which slowed his speed. He was staring at the arena floor and occasionally at the other contestants, which Nia knew would not help him strategically.

Garun, on the other hand, doggedly marched forward, despite being bent double, just placing one leg in front of the other. It wasn't elegant and it looked very uncomfortable, but it was moving him along at a steady pace, his balance secure.

As the front pack of racers reached the middle of the field, Nia felt a wave of nausea overcome her, and her headache returned, stronger this time.

Then the accidents began again. Some of the contestants toppled sideways, into the person next to them, knocking them over. Because the field was so spread out, not as many were caught in tangles, but quite a few dropped their stones and had to waste time picking them up again. Cephan was lucky; the mermyd next to him toppled left instead of right. Garun was narrowly missed, because he was bent so low, but he kept plodding forward. One poor mermyd girl fell with two stones colliding on top of her, and emergency physicians had to rush out to tend to her.

Dyonis came to the front of the box and stared out at the field. Then he put his hand on Nia's shoulder just as she reached up to rub her throbbing temple. "Are you all right?"

Nia looked into his eyes. And she knew. It was as if Dyonis were connected to her as intensely as to Ar'an— she could see the guilt and sense what he had just done.

I am not ill. This was not a coincidence. Magic was used to help Garun. Powerful magic. And Dyonis is responsible. "I'm feeling a bit dizzy," Nia said. "I think I'd better go home now."

Suddenly the water around her was filled with a roar. It was her family cheering.

"What's happening?" she asked, startled.

"Are you blind? Garun was the first to the pole!" her father shouted. He threw his arms up, cheering wildly.

Nia stared openmouthed at Dyonis, but he did not return her gaze. This time, Garun had won.

Chapter Ten

Nia swam toward the central Marketplace of Atlantis, angry, numb, and confused. She had not slept well. Her world was no longer what it seemed. *My grandfather is a cheat. And my parents, and the rest of my family—they're obviously involved as well. It must have been what they were talking about all those times when they grew quiet upon my arrival.* A new, sickening thought struck her. *The Councils are cheats too. Dyonis could not use so much power without them knowing. They intend to completely violate the trust of the citizens of Atlantis in order to make Garun an Avatar. But why?*

Nia had considered not showing up for the Third Trial. Why bother, if the Councils were going to ensure Garun's success? But her suspicions, strong as they were, had not been proven. Yes, she had been as certain as she'd ever been of anything when she looked in Dyonis's eyes yesterday. But that wasn't the same thing as tangible evidence. What could she do —announce to Atlantis what was happening?

Who would believe her? And if someone actually did, then what would happen to her grandfather? How could she do that to someone she loved so much?

Nia let her gills open wider to take in more oxygen, trying to clear her head. She had managed to arrive at the central plaza of the Grand Marketplace a little early. The shops right on the edge of the plaza were closed for the day. But others, on side streets, were doing a booming business. Spectators already crowded the balconies and terraces overlooking the Marketplace, and an area in one corner of the plaza had been roped off to keep the crowds clear of the contestants.

Automatically, Nia looked for Cephan, but apparently he hadn't arrived yet. She did spot Garun right away, though. He was hanging on the guardrope, impatiently cleaning the webbing between his fingers, looking like the completely ignorable nothing that he was. *What?* Nia wondered. *What quality does he have that is so precious that I don't have? He probably doesn't even know himself, the poor fool.*

Nia swam up to him. "Hello, Garun."

"Nia. You look awful," he replied without blinking.

"Good morning to you too," she said, barely restraining her annoyance. "I didn't sleep well last night."

"I told you to get a good night's rest, didn't I?" he reprimanded her.

"I had too much to think about."

"Don't you want me to win?" he demanded.

"Oh, you'll win. I'm surprised you have any doubts about that," she muttered.

Garun shrugged. "Anything can happen. So, I hear you're going to be taking over my position at the Archives."

Nia sighed. "Yes, I suppose so. My parents want me to."

Garun shook his head. "You're so lucky. I wish I didn't have to leave it."

Nia's eyes widened. "Really? Why?"

"I *loved* that job," he said. "In my opinion it's the best job you can have here in Atlantis."

Nia wrinkled her nose in disgust. "I don't know how that's possible," she said.

"You can learn about *anything* there," he insisted. "Anything you want to know about Atlantis, or even landdweller history, it's all there. If you know where to look. And they'll train you to know where to look."

Suddenly Nia had an idea, about a way she could learn the truth she needed to know so badly. "Anything? Even records of the Councils? And their decisions?"

Garun frowned. "Of course. That's what the Archives were originally set aside for. Everything written by an Avatar is stored there. All the meetings recorded, going back to the Sinking and maybe earlier."

"Have you read them?" Nia asked hopefully.

Garun rolled his eyes. "It's not like you can just pick them up and read them. They're stored in the dry room. And they're filed by code. You have to know what you're looking for. Which means you have to be a Council member yourself, or have specific instructions from a Council member."

"Oh," Nia was a little disappointed, but of course it wasn't going to be that easy. Still, it meant there *was* a way, possibly, to find out what she was desperate to know. "Thank you, Garun," she said. "You've given me reasons to actually look forward to working in the Archives."

"I hope so," Garun said. "I'd hate the thought of someone taking over that post who didn't appreciate it."

"Oh, I'll appreciate it," Nia promised. "I definitely will." Her attention was distracted as Cephan arrived with his second, a thin Stingray male Nia had seen only once or twice. Cephan saw her and waggled his eyebrows in greeting, but didn't speak. Contestants were not allowed to talk to competitors other than their teammates during the

Third Trial. Nia gave him a smile before he turned away to talk to his second.

The rope enclosure filled quickly with the rest of the contestants. The noise and energy from the surrounding spectators filtered down into the plaza. Workers of the Lobster Clan, in their bright blue-and-red tunics, handed each team a folded leaf of kelpaper. "Don't unfold until you're told," the workers said as the notes were passed out. "Teams who do will be disqualified."

Garun snatched the kelpaper out of the worker's hands and held it tightly.

Does he not trust me? Nia wondered. *Or is he just being his usual selfish self?*

Then Xemos came swimming out overhead, accompanied by the crowd's roaring and cheering. It began to sink in that she really was part of the Trials after all, even if only for a little while, and Nia felt some excitement stirring in her blood.

"Welcome, again, citizens!" Xemos announced. "Welcome and be witness to the Third Trial. In this test, those who would be Avatar must prove their ability to work closely with another, to pool their intelligence and strength to solve problems at hand. Each challenger has chosen a second, a teammate of their own clan, who will assist in finding the three objects each team must gather. While speed will be noted, we will also be judging cooperation and creative thinking. Each of the contestants will be given a clue on kelpaper. There is no exact answer to the clue—it will be up to the imagination of the competitors to select objects that satisfy the description.

"Each team will also be given a sailcloth sack. Competitors, please note the size of the sack—the objects you select must be able to fit into it. Therefore, you must not bring back anything bigger than your head. Please do not forcibly remove any object attached to a building or a person. We want Atlantis to remain in one piece after you are done. At the trumpet blast, you may open your clues for the first goal."

Xemos swam away, and the conchshell trumpeters emerged out onto balconies high above the square. Every team member gazed at the musicians, waiting. In one swift movement, the trumpeters raised the shells to their lips and gave a blast. Garun ripped open the kelpaper, and Nia read over his shoulder.

"Where are sea and mind contained,
Together flowing, together still,
A world that's guided by the will?"

"This one's easy," Garun said. "Follow me."

"What is it?" Nia asked.

"Not here. Do you want everyone else to know?"

So Nia swam after Garun as he swam at a casual pace north out of the Marketplace. He didn't seem to be in a hurry. A few of the other teams took off like sharks after prey, each headed in a different direction. The remaining teams hovered in the plaza, still puzzling over the clue. Some of the people standing on the balconies cheered down at them: "Bluefin! Bluefin! Garun! Garun!" But neither Nia nor Garun even glanced around to see who it was. It was considered bad form.

Garun brought her under a stone archway that led into a narrow, curving alley between tall clan palaces. Each layer of the palaces had family apartment branches, but there were few windows on the alley side. As Garun angled up and began to swim higher, Nia again felt the itching, touching in her mind—faint this time. *Oh no. The Councils aren't going to try to interfere in this Trial too, are they?* But it wasn't the same as the headaches and nausea of the day before—it was more like the infant Farworlder. Nia shook her head and chose to ignore it. It was too confusing. She didn't need the distraction right now.

Higher and higher Garun swam; then he veered

toward a specific palace, to the topmost apartment, where the clan elder would live. There he entered an open window bearing the design of the Octopus Clan.

"Garun!" Nia shout-whispered, "We aren't supposed to go into private homes!"

But he didn't even look back. Not knowing what else to do, Nia swam in after him.

The window led into a large, square room with shelves on the walls and a tall stone table in the center. Garun was taking a glass sphere the size of his hand off a pedestal on the table. "Garun!" Nia swam up to him. The sphere was hollow, like the toy float Cephan had given the little Farworlders. But this sphere had colored oils and sand swirling around within it.

"It's a meditation globe," Garun said. "It's used in magic training for focusing the mind to do basic telekinesis. This is my tutor's teaching room, so it's not really private at all."

Nia paused. *Is this part of the special training and help Cephan was hinting at?*

"But that must be incredibly valuable," she said.

"My tutor won't mind if I borrow it," he said with a shrug.

"But it must also be very rare—only a very few

contestants would be able to find such a thing. Isn't that a bit unfair?"

Garun whirled on Nia in exasperation. "What is the matter with you? First, anyone who studies magic seriously knows where to find versions of this—there are cheaper ones around. But you spent all your time on physical training instead of magical studies, so I suppose you wouldn't know that. And second, what do we care whether it's fair? We are trying to win here."

Nia stifled the angry comebacks she was dying to make. *Just play along*, she told herself *Maybe later, when I'm at the Archives, I can find proof of this unfairness and bring it to light. But not yet.* "I'm sorry," Nia said. "I had too much fair play pounded into me at the Academy. I'll try to let it go."

"You would be wise to," Garun said. "You have no idea how important this is. To everyone."

"Oh, I have some idea," Nia retorted.

Garun only looked at her, put the sphere in the sailcloth sack, and said, "Let's go."

Nia and Garun were cheered again when they reentered the plaza. Nia ignored it, feeling like they didn't deserve the praise. Garun signaled to the Trials worker that they were ready, and handed off the cloth bag. The worker dutifully took the bag and went off to log the item and the time. Then the worker returned with the bag, and the second clue. Again, Garun took possession of the kelpaper, and Nia had to read it over his shoulder.

> "Life contained,
> to sustain
> other life."

Garun rubbed his chin and frowned. Nia could not help thinking of Ma'el. That was surely "life contained," if anything was—and if Dyonis could be believed, Ma'el was confined in order to save land-dweller lives. But they couldn't very well bring Ma'el in.

"Food sustains life," Garun murmured. "But fish is already dead by the time we eat it. And what do they mean by contained? Food contained is already dead."

Nia remembered the Starfish warehouse—the fish that were sent up in the baskets were already dead. But then she remembered the baskets she saw the hunters and shellfish farmers bringing into the Lower Market. "Come on," she told Garun. "I know what will work, and where to find it."

"But—"

"Just come with me." A wild thought was growing in Nia's mind, and she wanted to get moving before she could talk herself out of it. She grabbed Garun by the elbow and kicked off out of the plaza with powerful strokes.

"Where are you taking me?" Garun asked, but he did not struggle from her grip.

"Be quiet," Nia instructed. "Do you want everyone to hear?" she said, turning his words on him.

She swam past the pearl shop where she had met Cephan days before, swimming in a circle around it until she was certain no one happened to be watching. Then she ducked down alongside the wall with the bubbling windows until she found the weighted drapery. Nia found the metal door in the wall.

"Hang on to me," she told Garun.

"What are you doing?" Garun nearly shrieked.

"Do you want to win or not?" Nia demanded, impatient. "Hold on, or else." Somewhat to her surprise, Garun meekly put his arms around her waist. Nia turned the scallop-shaped knob, muscled the door open, and swam in, pulling Garun in with her. The door slammed shut behind them.

Nia grabbed onto the metal rung beside the door, finding she had to hold on with all her strength. The roar of the bubbling water filled her ears. "Open your gills and breathe!" she yelled to Garun. She held on as long as she could, taking in the superoxygenated water. When she could no longer feel her fingers, she released the rung and let the current take them.

It wasn't as much fun as it had been with Cephan. Nia didn't really like being so close to Garun, who was making little cries of surprise and terror as the water propelled them down through the tunnel. She also had to pay attention to the phosphorescent markings along the wall to make sure she found the right door.

Soon Nia was running out of oxygen, and she knew she had to stop again, but now they were hurtling down the tube at amazing speed. By turning her feet, she was able to direct their movement over to the right-hand wall and as the next phosphorescent marker came by she reached out to grab a rung. But her hand banged hard against the metal, she couldn't grip it, and they rushed right past.

This was bad. Nia already felt herself wanting to go to sleep. If she couldn't grab a rail or open another door, she and Garun would go unconscious. Nia didn't know how long the tunnel was or what mechanism lay at the farthest end. Too long without oxygen, and she and Garun would both die.

Pulling Garun up closer, she yelled in his ear, "Garun, you have to help me! We have to grab the next rung!"

"Uhhhhh?"

Nia started to panic. Her heart beat loudly in her chest, and black spots started to appear before her eyes. She used what strength was left in her legs to get right beside the wall, letting it scrape against her skin. *This is going to hurt*, she thought, but she figured it would be better than dying. She held her arms out ahead of her. She felt metal strike her hands, and she gripped it for all she was worth. Her fingers began to slip. . . .

Garun's hand reached up beside hers. With three hands holding the rung, and Garun holding Nia's waist, they could withstand the rush of water current. Nia opened her gills and let the water rush by. The sudden energy was incredible, and she just hung there some moments, basking in the feeling of being awake, alert, alive. It was like returning from the dead. She looked up and saw the phosphorescent marker for a door. *We've got to get out of here*.

Hooking one foot into the rung, Nia felt along the wall and found the handle for the door. She turned it and shoved the door open. She and Garun swung around and grabbed the door frame and pulled themselves through before the current could carry them away again. Once they were outside the tunnel, Nia let the door clang shut behind them.

The water seemed terribly silent after the bubbling roar of the tunnel. The larger, bare corridor they were now in looked similar to the place where she and Cephan had left the tunnel, but Nia couldn't tell whether she had picked the same door.

"What an unusual mode of travel," Garun said, finally. "For a moment there, I thought you were trying to get us killed. Now can you tell me where we *are*?"

"We're in the Lower Depths," Nia said.

"Oh, joy. My favorite fun-time destination," Garun said. "Do you mind if I just float here and try to recover from nearly *dying* for a few minutes?"

"That's a good idea," Nia said. "That's a *very* good idea. You just wait right here, Garun, and don't move. I'll go get our object and be right back."

"We're not going to return that way, are we?"

"No, Garun, I promise. We're not."

"Good." Garun leaned against the wall and let himself sink, closing his eyes.

Nia took that opportunity to dash off, swimming as fast as she could down the corridor. She was in luck. It was the same door Cephan had used; she was in the same place. Nia passed by the tunnel that sloped upward to the Lower Market and hurried on through the disused, mossy corridor, until she reached the great circular door at the end. The one leading into Ma'el's cell.

Chapter Eleven

I must be crazy, Nia thought as she worked at the metal wheel to open the door. *He probably won't tell me anything. But it's my one chance. If I'm quick, I lose nothing. If he tells me, I could gain everything.* The trip through the oxygenation tunnels must have given her more energy than she thought—the door wasn't that hard to open. Nia swung the huge round door aside just far enough to slip in.

Nia ducked into the narrow room beyond and swam up to the half-wall with the wires stretched across the opening. She did as she had seen Cephan do—she plucked one of the wires. She felt her fingers sting and heard a noise go off somewhere in the room beyond. "Hello?" she called out. "Ma'el?"

The dark-bearded mermyd swam into view, astonishment on his face. "Well. This is an unexpected visit."

"I'm not staying long," Nia said, trying to keep her voice steady. Her heart beat rapidly, and she was sure her face and gills were pale from fear.

"No one ever does. Except for me. And my shadow." Joab swam up beside Ma'el.

After having been close to Ar'an, Nia could now see that Joab was very different—shadowlike and vaguely sinister. Nia would not want to be within tentacle reach of Joab.

"Have you come for a surprise inspection?" Ma'el asked.

Nia shook her head. "I've come to ask a question," she said, swallowing.

Ma'el blinked and raised his brows. "You wish to ask something of *me*?"

"It's something only an Avatar—or a former Avatar— might know."

Ma'el regarded her, narrowing his eyes. "Interesting. And you cannot ask it of any current Avatar, or of your *grandfather*?" he asked, placing a strange emphasis on the last word.

Nia shivered at the threat she felt in his tone, but shook her head, refusing to show she was afraid. "I need to find something in the Archives. I hear there's a code for how the Council's records are filed. I want to know how I would find any record of a secret meeting or decision made recently—right before the upcoming Ascension was announced."

A smile played around Ma'el's lips. "This is truly won-derful," he said. "The pride of the Bluefins wants to go delving into the Council's secret business."

"Will you tell me or not?" she asked, her throat tightening.

"How could I resist such a naughty request? You offer me the tiniest bit of revenge. But . . . there is a price."

Nia stiffened. There was no way she would agree if what he wanted meant danger to her family. "What price?" she asked.

"Information, of course," Ma'el replied. "I hear so little of the world above these days. And the fellow who has taken Cephan's place as my jailer since he left to compete in the Trials is tediously silent."

Nia let out a slow breath. She saw no reason why telling Ma'el what was happening in Atlantis could bring harm to anyone she loved. "I don't have much time," she reminded him. "What do you want to know?"

"How are the Trials going?"

Nia sighed. "The first two are over. Cephan won the first one."

"Ah, good lad. I knew he had promise. And the second?"

"Was won by my cousin Garun."

"Excellent. And . . . ah! I understand now. You are in the midst of the Third Trial, the treasure hunt. I remember it fondly. Which is why you are here with time short."

"*Yes,*" Nia said impatiently.

"I see." He paused, breathing bubbles in the water between them. Nia again found it hard to hide her shaking in his presence. "So you wish to have the code, then," he continued. She nodded. "Very well. What is the date again?"

"YA 5226, the twenty-fifth day of Warmingwater."

Ma'el paused and did some calculations on his fingers. "Ah. Given that secret meetings are very rare, I'll make the assumption it is the first one of this year. Therefore, you should look for . . . purple-blue-sixty-five. And do not ask for the formula; it would take too long to explain."

"Purple-blue-sixty-five," Nia repeated. "Thank you." She turned to go.

"Wait!" Ma'el cried.

Nia stopped. "What?" she said, her voice shaky.

"What clue are you on?"

Nia frowned, but the tension in her muscles eased slightly. "The second. Why?"

"Excellent. Just one moment."

Ma'el disappeared out of sight. Nia had just decided not

to wait when he reappeared, and he and Joab approached the low wall. Ma'el slipped something between the wall and the lowest wire. "For you. If I know my fellow Councilors, this should answer your third clue."

Nia cautiously approached the wall. The object was a tiny knife, clearly made by a land-dweller. It was all of gold, its hilt the shape of a female mermyd. "It's . . . lovely. But they'll ask where we got this."

"Tell them you found it behind Madame Hebe's Land and Sea Shop. They will believe you."

More cheating, Nia thought. But with so much irregularity, what was one little bit more? Nia reached in and grasped the knife.

Quick as light, Joab's tentacle slipped around Nia's wrist and held it fast.

"Let go of me," Nia said evenly, although her whole body was trembling in fear.

"Just some last words of wisdom from my Farworlder friend here," Ma'el said, putting his face close to the wires. "The Unis is strong, Niniane. It takes a sharp and wicked knife to cut the fabric of Fate and shape it to one's ends. The Councils are too timid for such tailoring of time. Therefore, what will be will be. But take heart, Niniane. For you are the knife. And great things will happen because of you."

Joab's tentacle slithered off her wrist, and Nia backed away until she hit the far wall.

"I've got to go," was all she could say, and she rushed out the door, Ma'el's laughter ringing in her ears.

Heart pounding, Nia slammed the circular door shut and swam as fast as she could down the mossy corridor. *It doesn't matter what they said*, she reminded herself over and over. *I got the code. Purple-blue-sixty-five. I have the code, and I don't care . . . but what did they mean that I am the knife? This little knife in my hand?*

She stopped swimming suddenly, trying to remember something. The second clue! Nia stuck the golden knife into the sharkskin pouch at her waist, then dashed up the sloping corridor to the Lower Market. The intense taste of fish and seaweed again filled her mouth as she swam out among the booths. She glanced around frantically and then saw what she'd intended to find—a merchant receiving baskets of live fish from hunters and shellfish from mussel farmers.

Nia swam up to the merchant so fast she startled him. "Niniane of the Bluefin Clan. I'm in the Third Trial. I'd like one of your small baskets of mussels, please." The rule was, a team could demand of any merchant in Atlantis an item for the Trial. The merchant would be reimbursed by the Lower Council later.

The fishmonger narrowed his eyes with suspicion. "Maybe you are and maybe you aren't. If you are, do you know how long it will take for me to get paid? Do you really think I can afford to just *give* you my wares?"

"I don't have time for this." Nia reached into her pouch, poking her finger on the knife, and pulled out two pieces of coral—most of her pay from the last month of serving in the nursery. "I have no wish to inconvenience you," Nia told the fishmonger. "Please accept this as payment."

His eyes widened as she placed the coral pieces in his palm. "Take as many as you like, my lady!" He thrust two baskets into her arms.

"Just one will do, thank you," Nia said. She turned and swam as fast as she could back down to the corridor where she had left Garun.

He wasn't there. "Garun!" she cried.

"There you are!" he responded from behind her.

She turned and saw he'd been hovering in a small alcove. "I told you to stay put," she said.

"You were taking too long," he argued.

"I had to haggle. But I've got it. Life contained two ways. See?" She held up the basket.

"That won't fit in our bag!"

Nia looked at it. "It will if we break off the handle. Come on!"

"Oh, it's too late. We'll never make it back in time. We're doomed."

Nia ignored him and started back to the Lower Market.

Garun squinched up his face as he tested the water. "What an amazing flavor you've discovered—"

"This way," Nia interrupted, leading him over to Spyridon's booth.

"You again," Spyridon greeted her. "And with a different young man this time."

"Please, can you give us a lift in your baskets?" she asked, hoping Garun hadn't heard that last remark.

Spyridon narrowed his eyes. "You seem to have mistaken me for being in a different line of business."

Nia was ready to pay with her last piece of coral, or perhaps give him the golden knife, when Garun cut in. "We're the Bluefin team for the Third Trial," he said impatiently.

"Well, why didn't you say so in the first place?" Spyridon asked. "Always wanted to be part of the Trials. Hop on in."

Nia breathed a sigh of relief and showed Garun how to

curl up in a basket. Spyridon gathered some other merchants, happily exclaiming that these were Ascension
contestants who needed assistance. With many hands to
pull on the ropes, the baskets containing Nia and Garun
rose swiftly up and up and up. Nonetheless, Nia heard
Garun's whining from the basket below her.

"We won't be in time. I should never have chosen you
as my second. I don't know why I let you lead me into
this."

"We're *fine*," Nia growled back at him. "We are going
to win. Stop worrying." She ignored the rest of his moan-
ing all the way to the Starfish warehouse.

The warehouse was deserted—everyone had gone to
watch the Trial. Nia clambered out of her basket, gazing
around.

"Where *are* we?" Garun asked as Nia helped him out
of his basket.

"Not far from home. Help me get the basket into the
sack."

They had to push the handle down and tug the sack
tight around the mussel basket, but they made it fit.

"There," Nia said. "Now, last one to the plaza is a sea
slug. Let's go!" Nia took the netting down from one of the
windows, carefully replacing it after she and Garun were

out. She caught up to Garun, and they raced at high speed
back to the plaza.

There was only mild applause for Garun and Nia as
they turned in their sack. When they asked their ranking,
they found that more than half the teams had already
come back.

"See?" Garun hissed at Nia. "We've lost. Let's just
hope we're not disqualified."

"It's only the second clue," Nia said. "We still have a
chance."

The Lobster Clan worker returned with the third and
final clue:

> "Land and Sea
> Eternity
> Death and Life,
> Beauty, strife."

"They warned me the third clue was tough," Garun
said. "Full of contradictions."

Nia thought of the knife Ma'el had given her. "He was
right," she murmured. "It fits."

"What?" Garun asked, his small eyes narrowing
further.

Nia leaned close to Garun's ear. "Where is Madame Hebe's Land and Sea Shop?" she asked.

"Over there, I think," Garun said, waving his hand in the direction of the far side of the plaza.

"Follow me."

"Oh no, not again!"

"No, this will be quick and painless, I promise," Nia assured him. She led Garun to the narrow passageway behind that row of shops. They were closed, fortunately, and Nia spent a couple of minutes pretending to rummage around in the trash bins.

"Nia . . ."

"Got it!" She returned to Garun and showed him the little golden knife. "It's made by a land-dweller, and the mermyd represents the sea. It's made of gold, which never rusts or rots—so it's eternal. It's an object of death with an image of life. A weapon with a beautiful design. It fits."

"But how did you . . . ?"

"Come on, let's hurry," Nia cut him off. She turned and headed back, Garun following her. As she swam, the pride in solving the riddle faded, and she realized she hadn't even *wanted* to win. How could she, when a win for Garun would hurt Cephan's chances? But instinct had made her try her best, despite knowing that this whole contest was being controlled anyway. At least now, with the information Nia had gained from Ma'el, she'd soon be able to know the real reason her grandfather was using magic to help Garun win.

Chapter Twelve

That evening, a small celebratory dinner was thrown for Nia and Garun by their families at the Bluefin Palace, even though there were four more Trials to come. They had easily won the Third Trial, given the speed and creativity with which they satisfied the third clue. It had made Nia a little sick that no one besides Garun questioned how Nia had discovered the knife so quickly. And even Garun had stopped asking how she knew where to look. Apparently Madame Hebe had confirmed that she had once owned a knife like that among her wares, but had lost it many years ago.

Nia's parents had given Nia a beautiful new blue-and-silver fish-scale gown, in gratitude for her helping Garun win, and so Nia wore it to the victory dinner. But she had a very strange feeling when she received it—as if it were payment for doing something wrong. She had helped Garun win the one trial for which he *didn't* seem to have been given magical assistance from Dyonis. She felt a terrible sense of guilt that she was now as much a conspirator as the rest of her family in an effort to hand Garun victory, taking it away from Cephan.

Nonetheless, Nia tried to keep her spirits up as she milled and drifted around the dining table with her relatives, feasting on shrimp balls and tuna. After all, she had important business to conduct.

She found her moment when she saw her mother and Dyonis conversing off to one side of the room. It barely even surprised her when they broke off their conversation as soon as Nia swam up. Yet again, there was something they were keeping from her. Nia no longer felt guilty about interrupting. "Mother, Dyonis, there's something important I'd like to speak to you about," she said.

"Then, by all means, let us hear it," Dyonis said.

"Yes, we have the ears of dolphins, as they say," Tyra added.

"I've been thinking about what you said, Mother, about considering my future. And I've come to a decision. You were right about the Archives post. It's important to my family and my career that I should accept it. In fact, I would like to start there right away. Tomorrow, if that can be arranged."

Both her mother and grandfather looked astonished, but pleased.

"I am very glad to hear of your newfound ambition," Tyra said, "but, dear, the Trials are still going on."

"I wasn't very comfortable during the first two Trials, Mother," Nia admitted. "And I'm sure that Garun will do very well whether I am present to cheer him on or not."

"That's wonderful, dear, but I also meant that the Master of the Archives will be watching the Trials as well. There would be no one in the Archives to interview or train you until the Trials are over."

All the better for me, Nia thought. *If I can get in there.* "Could I at least look around, get a feel for the place and the work?" she pressed. "Then I'll be able to give a much better impression when I'm interviewed."

Tyra glanced at Dyonis. "Well—"

"I think it's an excellent idea!" Dyonis said. "Balasai will be there, and he's a very capable fellow. He can show Nia the ups and downs and give the Archives Master a good report of her when he returns."

And you won't have me around to notice while you're improving Garun's chances, Nia thought with an edge of bitterness.

Tyra shrugged. "There you have it, then. Start whenever you like. I will send word on ahead so that this

Balasai will be expecting you. Truly, Nia, I am impressed with this new maturity you are displaying."

"Yes, Mother," Nia said, looking at Dyonis. "I feel as though I've had to grow up a lot recently."

That night, Nia slept better than she had in a long time. The following morning, she allowed herself to sleep late. Then, after a quick breakfast, she drifted over to the Farworlder Palace.

Before going to the Archives, Nia decided to look in at the Royal Nursery. She wanted to say good bye, in her own way, to the little creatures. She was going to miss them.

The palace was nearly deserted, since many of the clerks and ministers had gone to watch the Trials. The coral stone, marble, and malachite building, with its high, narrow columns and narrow archways, seemed dream-like--without the usual bustle of those doing the business of the High Council, it was silent and forbidding.

Nia swam the familiar route to the nursery. The little ones in their crèches were calmer than the last time she had been there, but there was a forlorn feel to the place. And there was one pillar with an empty crèche.

"Nia! What are you doing here? Congratulations on the Third Trial!" It was Oenone, of the Starfish Clan, who often took one of the other shifts. "Why aren't you at the arena?"

"Thank you. I have no doubt that my cousin will do well," Nia said. "Besides, these are the mental Trials. It's not as much fun to watch them get out of a locked room and through a maze, or to sit like a magistrate in judgment of some imaginary disputes."

"Depends on what you enjoy, I guess," Oenone said. "Don't you want to see how your special friend is doing?"

Nia sighed, wishing gossip didn't travel quite so fast in this city. "Cephan did respectably in the Third Trial, and I'm not worried for his chances either. Besides, I'm going to be starting in the Archives soon, and I wanted to learn more about the position while there aren't many people there to interrupt me. But I wanted to stop here first, just to have one last look."

"The Archives! There are never many people in the Archives, Nia. That's one of the first things you'll learn. But, as you can see, all is well here, at last. The little ones were upset for a while when their crèchemate was taken. There was no ceremony to it—a Farworlder came in, scooped up the squidling and its shell, and carried it out. I've always wondered how they know which one to pick."

"Yes. So have I," Nia said. "It's funny. The one they took—he was my favorite of all of them."

"How do you even know which one it was?" Oenone asked. "They all look the same to me. If someone were to shuffle them around from shell to shell, I would never know."

"It's . . . hard to explain," Nia hedged. "I'd better be going. Balasai should be expecting me."

"Well, I hope you enjoy your new position," Oenone said, shaking out her long reddish curls as she turned back to the infant Farworlders.

"Oh, I expect I will find it worthwhile," Nia said.

She left the nursery and swam cautiously through the hallways of the palace, although no stealth was necessary. Truly no one was around.

The Archives were tucked away in a far corner of the palace, near the edge of the Dome. Nia had only been there twice before, delivering brief reports about the nursery. An archivist would duly take them and file them away. Nia searched her memory to try to recall what she'd been told at the Academy about the storage of documents.

Writing was difficult to preserve in the underwater world of Atlantis. Kelpaper had a pulpy surface that was easy to inscribe upon, but it disintegrated quickly if it was not preserved. In the dry room attached to the Archives, however, documents could be dried, and if need be, copied by a scribe in waterproof ink onto tablets or tough papyrus. These tablets would then be coated with a sealant, some form of tree sap, also impervious to water. This way, even if the dry room was ever flooded, important records would be preserved. And a dry room was natural as secure storage—most mermyds would rather lose a limb than enter one.

Finally Nia found the Archives' marble archway embellished with carved scrolls and papyrus reeds—more evidence of the land-dweller influence on the Atlantean past. Nia swam in.

Balasai was in the center of the room, reclining on a slab of black stone, playing with a puzzle of seashells and string. The slab was ringed with cabinets, which Nia knew would contain minor documents. On the ceiling above him was a circular, gated hole from which a strange golden light spilled out. Undoubtedly that was the entrance to the dry room.

Balasai was about her age, and Nia had gone to school with him. He was of the Dolphin Clan, a respectable family of scholars, but Balasai had huge webbed hands and feet. He had been teased as a child, Nia remembered, as being more frog than fish. And he had an odd way of speaking that caused others to think him simple, though he was not. Nia felt some empathy for him, though she did not know him well.

"Greetings, Balasai!" Nia said cheerfully. "Here I am."

"Hmm?" Balasai sat up and studied her a moment. "Niniane of the Bluefin, yes?"

"Yes. I am here to learn what I can of Garun's position so that I may successfully and smoothly take his place."

"Hmm. Not much to know. Papers come in. We file them. Papers are requested. We find them."

"Yes, but I will need to know where everything is, so I can find them and file them when I have to," she said.

Balasai shrugged and hopped off the slab. He paddled over to one curved bank of file cabinets. "These are the Ministries. Medicine. Building. Justice. Planning. Water. All these temporary records. Over here"—he indicated a tall set of shelves—"Avatar writings. Poetry. Plays. Most of them not very good," Balasai added in an aside. "Over here"—he paddled over to a low bank of drawers— "financial records. Very dull." He pointed to a shelf stacked with scrolls. "Land-dweller histories. Very exciting, if you like violence. Over there, mathematics and scientific papers. Very interesting, if you can understand them. That's about all."

"And up there?" Nia pointed at the hole in the ceiling.

"Oh. Up there. The dry room." Balasai paused, watching for Nia's reaction.

She didn't give him one. "Government documents are stored up there, right?" she asked innocently.

"Mmm. You won't need to go up there, though. Master Alphenor files those. Only he knows the codes."

"How does he get through the gate?"

"The gate is locked. The key is here." Balasai pointed to a key hanging on a peg on the wall.

"Ah. Well. What else?"

"That is all," Balasai said, settling himself back on the stone slab and picking up his string-and-shell puzzle again.

"What did Garun do all day?" she asked, watching him work the puzzle.

"Read things," Balasai replied.

"You don't seem to be reading."

Balasai shrugged. "I've read everything already."

"But if there's nothing for you to do here, Balasai, then why are you here and not at the Trials, like everyone else?" Nia asked.

"Ah," Balasai sat up. "Someone might come, they said. Someone might need to leave a document at the Archives. We cannot close the Archives, they said. So here I am, even though no one has come. Except you."

"That doesn't seem fair," Nia said, letting her voice soften. "Particularly when your clan is doing so well. If I had known that my first visit might keep you from seeing the Trials, I would have postponed it."

"Ah, the Trials," Balasai sighed. "I wish so much I could be there."

Nia bit her lip. "Well, maybe you can," she said, as if the idea had just hit her. "I mean, I can stay and watch the place. It will be good practice for me. You could go out and see at least some of the Trials. I'll stay here and watch the Archives for you until you come back."

Balasai tilted his head and regarded her. "You haven't been given a final approval for the Archives yet," he said, hesitation obvious in his tone.

"But that's just a formality, right?" Nia said. "Besides, I served in the nursery. If I'm trustworthy enough to watch over the Farworlder infants, then I think I can watch some kelpaper."

Balasai thought it over, then nodded again. "I'll only leave for an hour. Maybe two. Then I'll owe you a favor." He got up and laid the puzzle down on the stone slab. "Maybe you can solve this puzzle while I am gone," he said with a smile.

I hope to solve another more important puzzle, Nia thought.

"Until I return, then," Balasai said. He launched himself up and was out through the archway faster than Nia would have imagined he could go.

As soon as he was completely out of sight, Nia grabbed the key and swam up to the gated hole. She wasn't used to mechanisms like this one, but after a couple of minutes of fumbling she was able to swing the gate down and aside. Steeling herself for the ordeal to come, Nia sucked water through her gills several times before gripping the sides of the hole.

She pulled herself up. Her head broke the surface, and water dripped off the side of her head. First she slid one arm over the edge of the hole, then the other arm. Then, with all her strength, she hauled herself up over the edge and into the dry room.

Nia lay on the floor for long moments, feeling so, so heavy. Her body felt as though it were a sack of sand. She blinked in the brighter light—in a dry room there could be lamps with flame, much brighter than the phosphorescence that lit the rest of the city.

She gave a cough, and water leaked out of her mouth. Her gasps were loud and echoed off the walls. She reached out and latched onto a metal chair that was bolted into the floor, Nia hauled herself upright and stood, her legs wobbling. *Keep knees bent,* she reminded herself, remembering how she'd been able to walk in a dry room years ago. *Make sure weight is supported and balanced.* Nia started falling forward, and she abruptly sat in the chair. She'd grown a lot since her last experience with a dry room and had more weight to keep balanced. *How do mouthbreathers endure it?* she wondered.

Nia gave herself some moments to let her sight readjust. She saw the cabinets lining the walls, all of them the same. *How will I find which one contains purple-blue-sixty-five?*

Then she noticed a stripe of color at the top of every cabinet. The trouble was, the light in the room had such a yellow tint, it was difficult to make out the exact color of the stripes. But they seemed to be in order, from light to dark. So Nia assumed if the last one was black or brown, the one beside it was likely to be purple.

Rather than chance a fall, Nia got off the chair and crawled on hands and knees to that cabinet. She opened it, and saw a series of drawers within, also labeled with colored stripes. She found the blue drawer and slid it open.

There was a stack of treated papyrus within. Nia carefully lifted out the one on top.

She began to read it:

ARCHIVAL REPORT OF THE 3395TH CONVENEMENT
OF THE HIGH AND LOW COUNCILS, AS TRANSCRIBED
BY THE ARCHIVIST AND SCRIBE TIREUS
IN THIS YEAR SINCE ARRIVAL 5226, MONTH OF
WARMINGWATER, 10TH DAY.

This meeting was held in secret, and the Councils forewarned that no word of these proceedings should be shared with other citizens.

This is it! It must be! Nia's hands shook, and her rasping breath became more ragged, but she read on.

The matter of immediate concern on the agenda was the terrifying visions received by the Farworlder kings after their recent deep meditation. When they entered the meditation to use their powers of seeing into the Unis, the Farworlder kings saw that death would stalk the byways of Atlantis, that its waters would grow still and its great halls become ruins. And some- how this danger would come from the new Avatar. Since the Farworlder kings' perception is limited in that only a few days ahead may be seen with any clarity, and only months with any sense of general prosperity or danger, no details could be discerned at that point.

What is troubling about the current crisis is that the time has come when the kings should be able to see clearly what the source of the danger will be in the days ahead. Yet they cannot. They claim that their visions are clouded, like muddied water. There appears to be some magic that is being used to obscure their perception—magic that is similar to that of the kings, but also very different. The Farworlders cannot see the source of this unusual magic, and therefore have no way to counteract it.

Therefore this secret meeting was convened to determine what action the Councils could take to avoid the fate seen in the visions. The decision reached did not come easily, but we can only hope that its wisdom will bear out, and when the Trials have ended and the new Avatar ascends, all will be

right. While it pains the Councils greatly to interfere in the Trials, it is essential that the natural
order be interrupted in order to ensure that any
who would have likely become Avatar will no
longer have that chance.

I do avow that the above has been faithfully
inscribed and that these kelpsheets shall be preserved and stored in proper manner with no other
eyes to see them until it is deemed appropriate by
some future Convenement.

Tireus
Senior Archivist and Scribe

Nia felt dizzy, and she carefully put the papyrus back
into the drawer. So she *had* been right. The Trials had
been interfered with, and it was all because the
Farworlders had foreseen some kind of danger that
needed to be averted. Ma'el's words came back to her.
You are the knife, Nia. She thought of how her family
had acted around her, even Dyonis—the one mermyd
she trusted more than anyone. They had seemed *nervous*
with her. And somehow that was why they hadn't chosen
her to compete to be Avatar. They had instead obviously
decided to use their magic to assist Garun in winning

the position. But still, why Garun? What did it all mean? And how could she—or any mermyd in Atlantis—possibly be a threat to their world?

Her breath started to come in harsh, racking sobs. Nia closed the drawer, closed the cabinet, and slipped into the cool, soothing water, letting her tears add a little more salt to the ocean.

Chapter Thirteen

Nia managed to compose herself and shut the gate over the entrance to the dry room before Balasai returned. But her feelings were churning like the maelstroms of the sea. It seemed forever until Balasai returned, but in fact he had been gone only a short time. "Couldn't get a good seat," was all he grumbled as an explanation.

"Well. I will see you in a few days, then," Nia managed to get out. *If I can stand to come back here.*

Balasai shrugged, going back to his puzzle. "Later, then."

Nia swam for home. The streets of Atlantis were largely deserted—everyone was at the arena, of course. *Just as well*, Nia thought. *I'd be scowling at anyone I met.* Mostly, at this point, she was angry. How could the Councils have kept this information from the citizens of Atlantis? How could Dyonis have kept it from *her*?

Nia stopped in front of the Bluefin Palace and decided she did not want to go home. It would be empty and

lonely, and she would only brood. Nia decided she needed
to find the one person who still believed in her, who
wouldn't lie to her. She needed to see Cephan.

*He'll be in the Trials now, but at least I can watch him,
and maybe I can catch him when today's events are over.*
Nia turned away and headed for the Great Arena.

But the gateway to the arena was shut and guarded by
Orcas. "Sorry, Miss," they told her. "We're full. We are
only letting people out. No one in."

Nia wanted to argue that if some were coming out then
there must be room for more to go in. But Orcas could be
stubborn and single-minded on the job, and Nia didn't
want to waste time.

She politely thanked the guard and then swam around
the curve of the Great Arena, keeping her eyes on the
arched portico until she saw what she was looking for—a
low, recessed alcove. There was a door within it labeled
WORKERS ONLY.

Well, Nia thought, *I'm a worker. I work at the
Archives.* Glancing around quickly and seeing that no one
was nearby, Nia turned the scallop-shaped knob and
entered. It was a dark, tiny room, probably a storage area.
After blundering about for a bit, feeling along the walls,
she found another door. This led into a larger chamber, a

space between walls and beneath the stands. Nia could hear the voices of the spectators overhead. Searching more, she found yet another door that led into one of the sloping tunnels that went up into the stands.

Nia came out among the stands and looked down at the field. She was in luck. She had come in near one end of the oval field, the end where those contestants who had already competed were gathered. From the number of mermyds lounging about, chatting with one another, she judged that the Fifth Trial must be almost over. The high rope rack on which contestants awaited their turn to speak had only two mermyds left on it. A third mermyd was drifting before the Avatar Selenus, who was asking the Question of Judgment. Each contestant was given a different problem on which to play magistrate.

"And so," Selenus was saying, her voice carrying throughout the arena, "a hunter comes to you suing against a kelp farmer who has planted in the areas where prey used to be plentiful. The prey will not live among the kelp, and the hunter is forced to seek prey elsewhere. What is your judgment?"

The contender replied, "The kelp farmer must give the hunter some of his harvest, in the same value as what the hunter has lost. . . ."

Nia didn't listen to the rest. She had heard lots of questions like that during her rhetoric classes at the Academy. She always thought the answers were so obvious.

Nia slipped down to the wall separating the field from the stands, leaning against it. She could pick out Cephan in the middle of the milling contestants, but he was too far away to yell to. She tried to catch his eye and wave. He didn't see her, but someone else did—a mermyd standing next to Garun who nudged him.

Garun turned and scowled at her. "Not now," he mouthed.

Nia sighed. Strictly speaking, since the Trial was still under way, she shouldn't be trying to talk to any competitor, but if their part was already done, what was the harm? Still, she found a corner between the edge of a riser and the access tunnel entrance where she curled up to wait.

Finally Selenus announced that the Fifth Trial was over. "Results of the winning finalists will be posted in the morning. However, I will now read the list of those six clans that have been eliminated: Dolphin, Anemone, Barracuda, Seahorse, Stingray, and Narwhal."

Well, Nia thought, *Balasai will be disappointed. Wait, did she say Stingray?*

"No!" Cephan cried from the field.

Nia flung herself to the dividing wall. Cephan was clutching his hair and staring up at the Dome. Other contestants went to him and patted him on the shoulders. They helped him off the field and toward the participant's entry tunnel right beneath where Nia was. But as he passed Garun, Cephan shot a very angry glare at him.

Oh, no—what happened this time? Nia wondered. *Well, if he's already disqualified, there's no reason I can't speak to him now.* She vaulted over the wall and swam down into the dark tunnel after Cephan.

"Go away!" Cephan shouted as she came near him.

"Cephan?"

"I said . . . Nia?" Cephan turned and blinked at her. "What are you . . . you shouldn't . . . oh . . ." He grabbed her and held her fiercely to him, obviously too emotional to use his usual polite restraint.

Nia relaxed against him, enjoying the feel of his arms around her even though she knew how painful this had to be for him. "I had to find you," she said. "I wanted to be with you."

His muscles tensed. "Did you know?"

"Did I know what?" she asked, confused.

"That I was going to lose?" he said, his voice rougher and angrier than she'd ever heard it.

"What? No, how would I have known that?"

Cephan sighed, then let go of her and turned away. "Sorry. It's just . . . your cousin. There are things . . . Nia, something isn't right."

"What happened?" she asked, dreading the answer.

He leaned down and spoke softly in her ear. "During the Fourth Trial, when the competitors entered the labyrinth, some of them became confused. Not much, not for very long. Just long enough so that Garun's time turned out to be the fastest. It was subtle, but I could tell. Someone was using magic."

"They were?" Nia breathed. *What do I tell him? What will he think of me if I admit I've known for a while?* "You have a magic sense, then, like I do."

"Not like yours, I don't think," Cephan said. "But I could tell. It even worked on me. I was making good time until, for a moment, I got disoriented. The sort of thing that's impossible to prove, you know?"

"Yes, it would be impossible to prove," Nia agreed. "Your word against the Councils'."

"Exactly." Cephan rubbed his face and neck. "Oh, well. As the saying goes, the hunter who takes too many fish today will starve tomorrow. Justice will be dealt in time." Cephan looked past her shoulder. "I'd better go. My family will want to talk to me. I'll see you soon, I promise." Cephan turned and abruptly swam away.

Nia blinked in hurt surprise. *What was that about?* She sighed and turned to swim back out of the tunnel. The way was blocked. By Tyra and Pontus.

"Mother! Father! What—"

"Garun told us you were here," Tyra said, crossing her arms in front of her chest.

Nia once more had thoughts of strangling her cousin. "Yes, I came to see how Garun—"

"I thought you were going to be at the Archives," Pontus cut in.

"I was, but there wasn't much for Balasai to show me—"

"I thought you agreed," Tyra said, "not to come to the Trials anymore."

Nia couldn't hold back her anger a second longer. *"Agreed?"* she burst out. "I never promised that I wouldn't come. Why shouldn't I show up here, if I feel like it? I have as much right to see the Trials as anyone! Except, of course, that you're trying to hide something—"

The edge of Tyra's hand sliced through the water, coming close enough to Nia's face to scare her into silence. Tyra's lips were a thin line, and her gills flared, tinged with red. "You will not take that tone with us. I will not listen to foolish, dangerous accusations."

She's afraid, Nia realized. Tyra's voice was sharp, but there was fear in her brown eyes. What did she know about all of this that had her so scared?

"Go home, Nia," Tyra said. "We'll talk later."

Nia swam past them and headed out of the arena, overwhelmed by anger and hurt. When she got to her sleeproom, she stretched the curtain tight across the doorway. And later, when her parents came home, she pretended to be asleep so they wouldn't talk to her. That night, she dreamed of being a wild mermyd, swimming in a wide, unbounded sea.

Chapter Fourteen

"Thank you, again, for letting me sit in the Sunfish box," Nia said. In defiance of her parents' wishes, Nia had come back for the last day of the Trials, the Sixth and Seventh. The day when the Avatar-to-be would be chosen. If her family and the Councils were going to go through with what they seemed to intend, Nia wanted to be there to witness it.

"What are friends for?" Callimar said with a smile.

The Sunfish observation box was in an even better position than the Bluefin, and on the opposite side of the field. The only way her parents would know she was there would be if they focused Dyonis's farseeing tube right at her. And Nia had worn a blue silk scarf over her silvery hair to make herself less recognizable, at least from a distance.

She had slept in that morning so she would not have to talk with her parents. Her mother had left a note of semi-apology pinned to Nia's doorcurtain.

Dear Nia,

    Some unfortunate things have been said. All we have done, we have done for the best. Please believe me. Be patient. Be calm. Amends will be made, in time.

Meaning that they want to keep me quiet until the Trials are over, Nia thought. *Well, I will keep my silence, because it would do me no good to speak out. But from now on, I do things my own way. If they can't trust me, I can't trust them.*

The Sixth Trial was a test of magical skill and was a favorite among spectators. The contestants, now down to only six, were allowed to demonstrate whatever skill they wished although it must be cleared by the Councils first.

The six competitors were lined up down the middle of the arena. They had been permitted to choose in what order they would compete. Nia already knew, because everyone was talking about it, that Garun had chosen to do his demonstration last.

It was a brave, and possibly stupid, choice. It meant that Garun believed he would outdo the previous five. To seem less skilled than the competitor who went before you was to earn disapproval from the spectators and, it was believed, the Councils as well.

The conchshell trumpets sounded, and Xemos appeared, treading water above the Speakers' Platform. "Welcome, Atlanteans, for this, the final day of the Trials. On this day our last competitors prove themselves, and on this day the High Council of Kings will choose who will be the next Avatar."

Never mind that he was chosen long ago, Nia thought with a rush of bitterness.

"The Sixth Trial, as you all know," Xemos went on, "is a demonstration of magic, of mental concentration through which a mermyd's thoughts can alter matter. Only the most skilled in this talent are appropriate choices for Avatar, for their power will be used in tandem with that of their Farworlder king, to make our waters flow, to anticipate dangers, and to keep our citizens healthy. Welcome, then, our last six competitors, who will attempt to impress and amaze us with their skill." As Xemos finished his speech, the arena fell silent.

"Helio of the Sunfish shall be first," Xemos intoned.

Naturally, Callimar and all her family moved up to the front of the box. "Helio, Helio," they all softly chanted, as if saying his name would help his conjuration.

Nia didn't mind if they blocked her vision now and then.

Helio was a beautiful fellow, with golden locks, a long, slim physique, and an elegantly shaped tail. He had never given Nia a second glance the few times she had met him.

Being the first competitor was a brave position, but not as much as last. You had to be good enough to be memorable throughout the competition, but the other competitors had to do better than your display.

Helio swam straight up, rising above the arena bed. He fluttered his tail gently, hovering a few mermyd-heights above the floor of the arena, and cupped his hands before him. As he frowned in concentration, a sphere of pale-green phosphorescent light appeared within his hands. The spectators around the arena oohed and ahhed. The sphere of light rose up, out of his hands, to spin and twirl before Helio's face. It was very appropriate, Nia thought, that the Sunfish candidate was re-creating an image of the sun in front of him.

He held the light steady for many long seconds. Then, with a heavy sigh, Helio spread his arms wide, and the sphere of light vanished.

Cheers erupted in the Sunfish box, echoed by cheering

around the arena. Even Nia cheered. It had, after all, been a fine display.

The next contestant was of the Sealion Clan, a small family of dwindling numbers, who had dense fur on their tails instead of scales. This mermyd did her display as a dance. She made scallop and clam shells do an intricate twirl around her, showing her precise control of many small objects.

Her performance was received with polite applause in the Sunfish box. Nia expected that Pontus was probably making some rude remark, which made her very glad to be where she was.

As the next three contestants, an Orca, a Seabass, and a Squid, performed, Nia curled up comfortably in her seat, a giant soft pillow in the shape of a sea anemone. She wondered what Cephan was doing. She wondered if she should even care anymore that her cousin was probably going to be an Avatar. It was said that youth was brought into the Low Council in order to allow new ideas to be heard, to allow the possibility of change. But now they would be choosing an Avatar in order to avoid change.

Nia was jolted out of her reverie as Callimar joggled her elbow. "Wake up, girl. It's your cousin's turn."

"Oh!" Nia sat up on her pillow and leaned out of the

box. She stared at Garun on the competitor's platform,
hoping he could feel her judgmental gaze upon him. He
had to know that he was being given magical help.

Garun began like Helio, rising up in the water—but he
wasn't using his legs; he just rose like an air bubble. Like
Helio, Garun held out his hands, and a phosphorescence
appeared between them. Then he arched his back and
spread his arms wide.

And the glowing light spread too, until it surrounded
Garun's body, spinning and growing brighter and
brighter. Soon images appeared within the light—whales
swimming and dancing around Garun; a kelp forest sway-
ing in tidal pool sunlight; a band of dolphins battling a
shark, a city glowing in the depths of the sea. It was
everything beautiful about undersea life, about Atlantis It
was a love song in light to the city.

The applause and cheers began even before the light
faded, and Garun sank slowly back to the arena floor. Nia
stared openmouthed. And then she realized—*I didn't get
a headache. I didn't get sick. No one helped him.* It was all
Garun.

The cheering from the Bluefins could be heard all the
way across the field. "Gar-*un!* Gar-*un!* Gar-*un!*"

All right, he had tutoring, Nia thought, *but he must*

have had the talent to begin with, or he could never have done that. He isn't quite a nothing after all.

Garun, Helio, and the Sealion were the contestants who remained for the Final Trial. Although, at this point, after Garun's amazing show, it seemed almost a formality.

"The Seventh and Final Trial," Xemos intoned, "may seem simple. Childish, even. And yet it sums up the thinking of the contestants, and we learn whether their hearts are in harmony with the philosophy of our Councils.

"It is a riddle, created by the High Council of Kings. The mermyd who can perceive the truth suggested by the words of the Riddle may truly consider himself or herself equal to those who now serve."

Xemos floated before the three finalists and intoned:

"What is more precious than all the pearls of the sea,
  That, at times, must be earned by its opposite,
  Yet is more than worthy of the price?"

"Rest," the Sealion said.

"Um . . . love?" Helio guessed.

"Peace," Garun replied without hesitation.

A moment passed, and then Xemos swam over to

Garun and held up his arm. "May I present to Atlantis the one who is chosen to be the new Avatar! Garun of the Bluefin!"

What a surprise, Nia thought, shaking her head. But she was no longer so bitter. Even with all the help given, Garun had worked hard to achieve his victory. *While the Bluefins should be ashamed of some of the actions taken, they should still be proud of Garun.* Nia raised her hands to clap and felt her eyes grow warm with tears.

Every Bluefin was required to attend the congratulatory dinner that night, so Nia's parents couldn't even try to convince her to stay home. Still, Nia was determined to be on her best behavior.

The Meeting Hall of the Bluefin Palace was dazzling. Lamps with blue-purple chemical flames hissed and sputtered along the wall. Nia had never seen fire underwater, and she wondered if perhaps again the Councils were lending their magic to this special night.

A school of Bluefin tuna had been brought in for the occasion, and the huge, confused fish blundered about up at the roof of the hall. A band consisting of a trained singing pilot whale, two porpoises, a mermyd percussionist, and two horn players made merry, if chaotic, music. A squad of trained octopi lined one wall, shifting the patterns of their tentacles and bodies to form geometric designs, and changing the colors of their skin to match the mood of the music.

Everyone was dressed in finery, sharkskin and pearls and sea-dragon scales—some had so weighted themselves down with jewelry that they had to stroll the floor like land-dwellers. It looked very strange. Garun was at the center of all of them, of course, dressed in flowing robes of silver tetra scales and fringe dyed indigo with octopus ink. He was grinning and held his arms out expansively, telling all what he would do for Atlantis now that he was going to be an Avatar.

Nia sucked in a deep breath through her gills and walked right up to Garun. The crowd around him grew silent and watchful.

"Congratulations," Nia said with a nod of her head. "I mean that. You bring honor to our clan."

The mermyds around her relaxed visibly and smiled.

"Thank you, cousin!" Garun said. "And I mean that. Your goodwill is important to me."

"Your display in the Sixth Trial was amazing," Nia said. "I had no idea you had such magical talent."

A smug grin filled Garun's face. "I'll bet Balasai didn't

show you where the magic scrolls are kept. That's because they are mostly under my desk. Well, what used to be my desk. I'd been studying them for years. You might take a look at them yourself, sometime."

"Ah. Yes. I just might. Thank you," Nia said. Having expended about as much goodwill as she could stand, Nia made a polite exit and found a corner of the room to be unnoticeable in. She watched the attention paid to Garun, and an odd thought occurred to her. *What if the Councils made a mistake, and Garun is the Avatar who will bring about destruction?*

But something had to have convinced them otherwise, even if the document she'd read hadn't said exactly what.

Sala, dressed in bright, frilly pink, came swimming up to her. "Lady Niniane?"

"Hmm? Yes?"

"I have a message for you." Sala handed her a folded piece of kelpaper and swam away.

Nia unfolded it. And her heart leaped. It was from Cephan.

Dearest Nia—
  Meet me by the servants' entrance.
                                C.

Nia scraped the pulp off the kelpaper with a fingernail so that the message was destroyed. Then, making sure that her parents' attention was completely on Garun, she headed down to the servants' entrance at the back of the Bluefin Palace. Now she was glad she was wearing the blue-and-silver gown, so that Cephan would see her in it.

She slipped outside into the darker, cooler water. "Cephan?"

A hand gripped her arm and pulled her into the shadows. She blinked, and as she opened her eyes she could barely see the outline of Cephan's handsome face. "Did anyone see you come down?" he asked.

"No, I don't think so," Nia said. "But honestly, I don't really care. Do you?"

Cephan shook his head. "How are you holding up?" he asked.

"It's all ridiculous," she muttered. "But Garun is the new Avatar-to-be. I've decided it's time to focus on my own life. I'm going to make some changes."

"I'm happy to hear that," Cephan said, breaking into a wide grin. "In fact, I have a suggestion for a change you might begin with."

Nia grinned back at him. "Do you? What is it?" she asked.

Suddenly, before she knew what was happening, Cephan was leaning toward her, and his lips were pressing against hers. Nia froze in shock for a second, and then returned the kiss, the pain in her heart turning to joy.

Cephan pulled back after a moment. "Is this . . . all right?" he asked gently.

Nia nodded. "It's perfect," she murmured.

Cephan let out a laugh, then pulled her into a tight embrace. "You have turned a terrible day into the best one ever, Nia," he told her.

"And you've done the same for me," she replied, meaning every word. Now that she knew Cephan shared her feelings, everything else faded away. She had longed for this moment for so long, and it was here at last—even if right now Garun was living the other dream she'd had for herself.

Cephan squeezed her again, then let go. "I don't want your family to start worrying," he said. "You should probably get back to them. I can see you tomorrow."

"Yes, of . . ." Nia stopped, frowning. "No, I can't see you tomorrow," she said. "I'm sorry, but it's the Naming ceremony. I have to be there, and you won't be . . . wait a second," she said, cutting herself off once again. "Maybe you can come with me!"

Cephan gave her a nervous glance. "I have a feeling my presence would be strongly discouraged at the Farworlder Palace doors."

Nia thought a moment. "So then I'll sneak you in," she suggested. "After the ceremony has begun, so that no one will dare cause a scene over it. You know all the secret entrances, so I can meet you at one of them."

Cephan rolled his eyes. "Servants' doors are not secret entrances, Nia. They just aren't usually noticed." He paused, considering her offer. "Well, all right then, if you think it's a good idea," he finally said. "Meet me at the lowest level, north door—it is the one nearest the Dome. It will be easiest for me to wait near without being seen."

"I will." She kissed him again, a long, slow kiss that warmed up the water around them. "Until tomorrow," Nia whispered.

"Until tomorrow," Cephan said, clearly reluctant to let go of her hands.

Nia smiled and went back inside, finding herself much more cheerful through the rest of Garun's party.

The following morning, Nia happily joined the procession that began at the door of the Bluefin Palace. All of Atlantis lined the streets and byways between there and the Farworlder Palace to show respect for the new Avatar-to-be. Garun sat on a palanquin made of carved, gilded hardwood that had come from a land-dweller sunken ship of ages past. It would he carried by six mermyds and towed by four dolphins. On Garun's lap, in an opalescent nautilus shell, sat the infant Farworlder prince to whom Garun would be mentally joined during the Naming. Nia had tried, on a whim, to send a mental *Congratulations* to the Farworlder infant, but she had no idea whether the message was received. She did sense that the poor little creature was nervous. Well, who wouldn't be, with such a crowd around it?

Nia was permitted to swim behind Garun's palanquin wearing her Nursery Guard bandolier, as part of the Bluefin Clan honor guard. She was able to wear a big smile as well, no longer upset by Garun's ill-gotten victory. She had something far more precious—Cephan's love. And it would all be worthwhile when she saw her parents' faces when she later escorted Cephan into the Naming ceremony.

Farther back in the procession were palanquins carrying the Avatars and their Farworlder kings. The Avatars sat motionless, their eyes closed, concentrating their mental energies on protecting Garun and the prince, and perhaps already working changes on Garun's blood so that he would not die when receiving the toxic fluids from the Farworlder prince during the Naming. Nia could sense pressure waves in the water around Garun's palanquin, making her skin tingle.

Dyonis was positioned at the front of Garun's palanquin, carrying the Sword of Peace, Eikis Calli Werr. It struck Nia how he'd had the sword out before any of them had known a member of their clan would be chosen. How had she not put it all together then? Dyonis had brought the sword out because he'd *known* he would need it for the Ascension.

The procession surged forward, moving slowly. Atlanteans on balconies overhead dropped silver fish scales, so that the water glittered and shimmered. Shell horns sounded, and mermyds sang and cheered.

For nearly an hour, the procession wound through the city. At last they came to the enormous double doors of the Farworlder Palace Great Hall. They were made of volcanic pumice stone, ribbed with whalebone ivory and studded with gold. The doors swung slowly inward, and the procession, all those who were permitted, entered.

Nia had never been in this part of the Farworlder Palace, as the Great Hall was reserved entirely for major events of state. During the days before the Sinking, this was where land-dwelling kings, emperors, and ambassadors would be received and entertained. She'd heard many stories of the strange, silvery metals found on the walls and floors here, remnants from the Farworlders' spaceship that had long ago landed in Atlantis. She was amazed to see for herself that the metals—synthetic substances from the Farworlders' original home—truly hadn't rusted or corroded over the years. Down the center of the floor of the enormous hall was a rectangular depression that had been a reflecting pool. Now it contained, at the far northern end, a throne of polished black basalt. In front of the throne was a pillar with a depression in the top, the right size to hold the shell of the Farworlder prince.

The hall was two stories high with a flat ceiling. Marble pillars decorated with inscriptions of the Farworlder language divided the sides of the hall. It was said that the inscriptions were part of a sacred book of the Farworlders, either containing their history, or a treatise on how to use their magical powers, or a description of how to find their homeworld in the vastness of the Greater Ocean beyond Earth, depending on who was telling the story.

There was a second gallery overlooking the Great Hall, faced with a row of smaller pillars and arches. Up into this gallery swam the High and Low Councils—the mermyds resting themselves on kelp rope cradles, the Farworlder kings floating above or behind them. Nia's gaze drifted to the retiring Avatar and king, and she wondered how this ceremony felt for them—knowing that it would be their last as Council members.

The clans of all the Low Council were represented, as well as all of the Bluefins. They swam, slow and orderly, into the Great Hall in near silence. If anyone spoke it was in low voices—others merely signed at one another. It gave a majestic feel to the occasion, and even Nia, despite her new cynicism, could not help but feel a little awe.

Rope lattices hung around the periphery of the Great Hall, and onto these the assembled nobility of Atlantis arranged themselves. The Bluefins would be reclining at the north end, nearest the throne where Garun would be sitting. Also, to Nia's relief, nearest a door by which she could make a quick exit to head down to the servants' entrance. Nia found a position on the rope lattice toward the back. Fortunately, her parents were expected by tradition to be at the front along with Garun's parents, and therefore they would not be able to keep an eye on her.

Garun's palanquin was set down beside the black stone throne. Garun's eyes were closed in deep concentration, his hands clasped tightly in front of his face. Two of the young Bluefin cousins picked him up off the palanquin and set him on the throne.

The Farworlder's shell was nestled into the depression in the column. Little pink tentacles waved slowly out of the shell. *Poor thing*, Nia thought. *It's poisoned.* For the past twenty-four hours, the Farworlder prince had been coaxing its body to make the toxin for the joining. The creature would have to release the toxin soon, by injecting the oculus secretion into Garun's palm, or else it would die. Nia wistfully wished she had given the little alien prince a name, but that was not her right to do. *Garun must give him a name now.*

The palanquins and other trappings of the procession were cleared away. The last of the processioners arranged themselves on the rope lattice. Dyonis swam slowly down the reflecting pool, still holding the Sword of Peace. He stopped before the pillar on which the Farworlder prince lay.

"Welcome, all, on this day of rejoicing," Dyonis boomed out. "For it is on this day that renewal comes to the leadership of Atlantis. It is on this day that a mermyd chosen of the best that Atlantis has bred shall Ascend to become an Avatar, and a new king, chosen as the best of its kind by the High Council, shall be Named. These two will be joined and take their place among the Councils of Atlantis to lead us into a new age, informed by their wisdom, their honesty, and their youthful enthusiasm.

"Garun of the Bluefin, are you prepared?"

"I am." His voice was thin, and Nia thought she detected a hint of fear. *Be strong, Garun,* she willed him. *You can do this.*

Dyonis turned to look up at the gallery. "Is the prince prepared?"

"It is," the Low Council chanted back as one voice.

"Then let it begin." Dyonis raised the sword above his head.

The Low Council of mermyds in the gallery began chanting a low drone on a single note. The water in the Hall vibrated with the sound, and Nia's skin hummed and tingled. Soon Garun and the prince were bathed in an unnatural, golden-green magical light—the combined power of the two Councils focused entirely on them.

It would take nearly an hour for the Councils to change the blood of Garun and the prince enough so that the oculus toxin could be tolerated and shared.

I must go get Cephan now, while everyone is distracted, Nia thought. But it was difficult to leave the sight of Garun suffused with the golden green light. With an effort of will, she detached herself from the rope lattice. She swam down behind it, along the wall of the Great Hall, until she reached the small side door.

Her skin still shuddered from the drone and the energy, and her body was sending her signals that something was wrong. Her heart was racing, and she was finding it difficult to get sufficient oxygen through her gills. But then, she had never been in the presence of so much magical power before. *I am sure the Councils know what they are doing.*

As quietly as possible, Nia opened the little side door. It led into a narrow corridor and a long flight of steps that went down. It showed the age of the Great Hall that the land-dweller stairs still existed as part of the building. Nia swam down and down, unable to shake the strange feeling. She was getting a little sleepy too.

The flight of steps ended at a large, bare room that showed signs of having been used recently for storage, although the mosaic floor hinted that it had been originally intended for grander purposes. It seemed to Nia to take forever to swim across it to the north door at the other side. *Why am I so weary?* she wondered.

Nia slid back the wood bolt from the door and pushed down on the golden latch. The door swung open, and cool water drifted in. There was a dim tunnel beyond, the stone overgrown with seamoss. No one was there.

Nia swam out through the doorway just a little. *Am I too early? Was he not able to get here? Did some pushy Orca stop him? Should I wait for him? How long?* She really didn't want to miss much more of the ceremony.

The water seemed deathly still and cold. Nia's skin started to creep. She was about to turn back and go inside when a dark shape entered the tunnel ahead.

"Cephan?"

"Not exactly, my dear."

Nia froze. It was Ma'el.

Chapter Fifteen

"A pleasure to meet you again, Lady Niniane," Ma'el said. "Of course, you remember my companion, Joab?" An ink-black shadow with eyes and tentacles loomed up behind Ma'el.

"Where is Cephan?" Nia demanded.

"Attending to other business, I believe. May we enter?"

Weary and anxious and frightened as she was, Nia still knew her duty. Even though she had guarded only the Royal Nursery, she was still a palace guard by training. Extending her arms and legs to block the doorway, she said, "You may not pass."

"Ah. I regret that we must be forced into rudeness. Joab?"

The Farworlder flowed forward, wrapping its tentacles around Nia's arms, legs, and torso. Its tentacles were strong enough to crack her bones if it chose. She felt its hard, sharp beak pressed against her stomach—not doing damage, but in a threat that it could. With hardly any effort at all, Joab detached Nia from the doorway and pushed her inside.

Ma'el swam after, closing the door behind him and throwing the bolt across it. He was idly turning a crank on a strange mechanism strapped to his chest.

Nia started to see black spots before her eyes, and her gills were stretching and fluttering, trying to find oxygen. "Wh-what are you doing?" she asked.

"What I have to do," he said tightly. "I am righting a great wrong."

"You . . . you were . . . interfering with the Trials!" she cried, wondering whether her guess had been wrong after all and this had all been Ma'el's work somehow.

"I? Oh, no, that was mostly the Council's doing," he replied, sending her heart sinking again. "Although I tried my level best to help my chosen candidate, I was outdone. Thus I am forced to implement my backup plan." He swam over to her and looked her right in the eye.

Nia shivered. "Backup plan?" she echoed.

"Did we not say great things would come of you, Niniane?" he asked, his voice low. "Did we not say you were the knife?"

"You're wrong!" Nia growled. "I would never do any-thing to bring harm to Atlantis or my family!"

"Your family," Ma'el said, then chuckled. "Do you really know who your family is, Niniane?"

Struggling against her fading strength, Nia said through gritted teeth, "My father . . . is Pontus of the Bluefins. My mother . . . is Tyra, born of the Seabass. My grandfather is Dyonis . . . of the Bluefins."

Ma'el shook his head. "I'm sure that's what they wanted you to believe all these years."

Nia felt another chill pass through her. "You're lying," she said. "Whose child would I be if not theirs?"

Ma'el sighed. "We had such dreams, long ago, Dyonis and I. We were so idealistic. His idealism took a different shape than mine. He wanted peace with the land-dwellers. I knew that would never succeed. Nonetheless, when our hunters brought in a woman they had rescued who had fallen off a sinking ship, Dyonis was quite taken with her. He decided to make his peace-making personal. Alas, she did not thrive, and she died soon after the child of their union was born. That child was you."

Nia blinked, unable to believe what Ma'el was saying. "Dyonis is my *father*?" she said.

"It was a not very well-kept secret in the Councils, but for Dyonis's sake, it was not bandied about. You were given to Pontus and Tyra for adoption, and no more was said about it."

Nia thought for a long moment. Dyonis had always been interested in her, patient and caring. Closer than most grandfathers-who-are-Avatars would be. But why was she even listening to this? Ma'el was a *criminal*. He was lying to her, of course.

"Why are you telling me these things?" she demanded. "Even if it's true, then why do you care?"

"Because, my dear, as Dyonis's best friend at the time, I had to give you a suitable birthing gift. One even Dyonis himself would never have had the courage to give you. I couldn't help tinkering. I put a tiny bit of oculus in you. Right there." He tapped her forehead. "That is why you have the powers you do. That is why you are special. In a way, I am your father too."

"No!" Nia cried. She tried to struggle, but Joab's grip tightened, making it even harder for her to breathe. It was all real now, impossible to deny. This was why she had those special powers, the ones no one ever believed in. It was why she could feel the Farworlders' touch, and why she'd been sick from Dyonis's use of magic during the Trials.

The distant droning of the Councils had dwindled

away. The water was now very still, very silent, very cold.

Ma'el's expression darkened. "It's time," he said, his tone serious. "I wish we could have . . . I wish this could have been different." He gestured at Joab, and the Farworlder released her.

As they swam away, Nia wanted to chase them, but she had no energy left. She could not move. Her gills fluttered but drew in no oxygen. The room darkened before her eyes, and she drifted into unconsciousness.

Nia was shaken awake, hearing Cephan's voice by her ear. "Nia! Nia! Are you all right?"

She felt water moving past her gills, and she sucked in the freshened water for a while before speaking. "Cephan? Cephan!"

"Oh, thank the gods!" Cephan cried. "Here, put this on." He slipped a collar of tubes made from perforated kelp stalks around her neck and strapped a box around her torso. "Here, turn this crank. It will help you breathe." He placed her hand on the mechanism.

"What is it?" she asked weakly.

"Turn the crank. It moves a set of paddles that push water through the tubes and past your gills. It's emergency equipment in the Lower Depths. All the filtration tubes and oxygenation tunnels have been shut down. The water in Atlantis is still."

Nia knew the danger of still water to a mermyd. "Everyone will suffocate and die!"

"Not everyone. Some of us have these, and we can escape."

"We can't just run away!" Nia protested. "We've got to stop Ma'el. How did he get out of his cell?"

"I don't know. I wasn't his guardian anymore, once I became involved in the Trials. I don't know who replaced me. Nia, he's stronger than either of us. There's nothing we can do against him."

"But he's not stronger than the Council. We have to go see if they're all right. And Garun. And the prince. And my—oh, come on, Cephan!" Terrified at what she might find, Nia swam back up the stairwell, up toward the Great Hall. She had to turn the crank on her chest frantically to get enough air.

"Nia, be careful!" Cephan shouted behind her.

She shoved open the little door at the top of the stairs. It was still silent in the Great Hall, and there was a taste of blood on the water.

Mermyds drifted, asleep and unconscious. Up above, at the ceiling near the gallery, the Farworlder kings of the

High Council drifted, spears through their bodies, dead.

Nia wanted to scream, but she held back and steeled herself for what she must do. She swam slowly behind the rope lattice, watching for Ma'el or Joab. *But who killed the kings? Who shut down the water flow? Ma'el has help, but from whom?*

When she saw her mother drifting in the lattice, Nia could not stop herself. She swam to Tyra and shook her. "Mother, wake up! Are you all right?" But her mother didn't stir. Nia tried placing the collar of her bubbler near her mother's gills, and she turned the crank. But Tyra didn't move.

Nia felt the tickle in the back of her mind again. But this time it grew into full contact. *Nia. Garun lives. Find us. We are behind the wall hangings.*

Not pausing to consider how this was possible, Nia swam to the tall weighted tapestries at the east end of the Great Hall. Cephan joined her, and together they pulled aside one of the tapestries that covered an alcove. Garun, the princeling, Dyonis, and Ar'an were huddled all together. Dyonis and Ar'an were using their magic to keep the water moving around them. Garun, while alive, was looking very green. The Farworlder prince was tucked tightly in its shell. Dyonis's Sword of Peace had dark bloodstains on the blade, steadily fading as the water washed them away.

"What luck!" Cephan said. "We have to get them to safety." Cephan reached for the Farworlder's shell, but Garun pulled it close to his chest.

"The Naming . . ." Garun rasped, "is not finished. We must complete the Naming."

Or he and the prince will die, Nia thought. "Where can we take them?" she asked.

Cephan thought a moment. "There's a filtration tube not far from that north servants' entrance. There will be some water flow in there from Outside, so the old man won't have to concentrate on moving water."

"Isn't that a rather dangerous place to hide?" Dyonis asked, frowning at Cephan. He shifted in place, and Nia tasted blood on the water again. Dyonis had been wounded, she realized with a sick feeling.

"The fact that it's dangerous means no one will look for us there," Cephan replied. "Stay put. I'm going to see whether the way is clear. I'll be back in just a minute." Cephan took off as fast as a mermyd could go.

Nia crouched down beside Dyonis. "Grandfather, are you all right?" she asked him, her voice trembling. It didn't matter at that moment if Dyonis was her father or grandfather, or even that he had withheld the truth from her. He was still the caring adult who had seen her through childhood and whom she loved more than anyone.

"If I can get some time and some quiet, I can heal," Dyonis said. "It is strange, so strange. . . ."

"What is?" she asked.

He heaved a deep breath. "The Farworlders had a vision—that the next Avatar would somehow bring disaster to Atlantis," he said, obviously straining to speak. "We were so certain that you would win the Trials if you competed that we kept you out of it, thinking it would help avoid the fulfillment of the prophecy." He paused, giving her a sorrowful glance. "Nia, I'm so sorry," he said. She shook her head, letting him know she was no longer angry. "We decided, instead, that we would choose the candidate of all the clans who seemed least able to pose any threat." He gazed over at Garun. "Garun had no desire for power," Dyonis explained. "And so we . . . helped him win. Little did we know the disaster would occur anyway. Though Garun himself did not bring it. Oh, Nia, we have wronged you and the people of Atlantis terribly, terribly. Will you ever forgive me?"

It struck Nia with full force then. She was to be the

Avatar. And she *had* brought the disaster. She choked back a sob. "I'm afraid I'm the one who needs your forgiveness," she said softly.

"What?" Dyonis narrowed his eyes in confusion.

"I let Ma'el in here," Nia confessed. "I didn't mean to. I thought it would be Cephan. And there's more—I spoke to Ma'el, before you mentioned him to me. His Farworlder touched my mind. I think they did something to me. Oh, Dyonis, it *is* all my fault!"

"Do not blame yourself, Nia," Dyonis said. "The Unis is strong, and it will have its way, just like a wave crashing on the shore. By choosing Garun, we were going *with* the Unis, not against it. The fault is ours for not seeing clearly. You were caught in the middle."

Just then Cephan returned. "All right, the way is clear," he said. "Let's go."

"We must see to Garun," Dyonis said. "Once the Naming is complete, it is then possible for us to apply our powers to greater problems. Help me up, young fellow." Dyonis extended an arm to Cephan, who hesitated, then took it. Dyonis awkwardly sheathed the sword in a scabbard at his side.

"Strange that a sword of peace should have to be used as a sword of war," Nia murmured.

"As the riddle that Garun accurately solved implied," Dyonis said, "sometimes the price of peace is war."

"This way," Cephan instructed. He guided them out of the Farworlder Palace Great Hall and led them toward the edge of the Dome. All around them lay the silence of the tomb. Mermyds floated, sleeping, drifting among the buildings. If the water didn't begin flowing soon, the sleep would turn to death.

"You were in the Trials, weren't you?" Dyonis asked Cephan. "Did rather well, as I recall." Dyonis looked at Ar'an, who seemed to be signing with his tentacles, although Nia could not read the gestures.

"I do not think this is the time to speak of such things, sir. We must hurry before Ma'el returns. Come along."

With Cephan guiding Dyonis, and Nia and Ar'an guiding Garun, who was clutching the Farworlder prince, the six of them made their way hurriedly toward the great crystal curve of the Dome.

The sea beyond the Dome looked dark and uninviting. Shadowy shapes drifted among the rocks below. Here and there, smoke plumes marked the presence of steam vents. Glimmering lights from deep-sea fishes and jellyfish, hydras and glow-shrimp, twinkled in the distance.

Garun's legs stopped moving, and Nia pressed her

shoulder closer to his neck. She worked the crank of the bubbler to get more air to him, and he seemed to perk up a bit. She didn't know what she could do for the Farworlder prince, still huddled in its shell. Its skin was now gray instead of pink.

Nia fell silent. Her whole world was coming apart, her present and her past. *But if I am to have any future*, she thought, *I must concentrate on the now. I must see Garun through the Naming safely, and then I must help Cephan and Dyonis wake up Atlantis, so that we can defeat Ma'el. Somehow.*

Cephan led them all to an opening—clearly the beginning of an oxygenation tunnel that had diverted some of the circumference current down to the Lower Depths. Nia was about to protest, then realized it would be foolish. The water flow was shut down—there would be no wild ride.

Instead, it was a long, dark journey, swimming down and down. The only fear was that whoever was helping Ma'el, or Ma'el himself, might appear.

At last, Cephan opened a door in the tunnel and helped to guide everyone out.

"Is it far?" Nia asked. "I'm not sure how much longer Garun can continue."

"It's right here." Cephan pointed at a large, circular gate covered with a fine mesh screen of net. He swam over to it and hauled on a lever of whalebone. The gate swung open. "Get in. Hurry."

Ar'an and Dyonis swam in first, Nia and Garun next. Cephan swam in last and pulled the gate shut behind them.

It was terribly cold in the filtration tunnel. Even though its mechanisms ran on steam from vents below, the dwindling warmth in the pipes could not offset the chill of the ocean depths. The water was fresher and easier to breathe in, but still not as breathable as what Nia had been used to all her life.

At the far end of the filtration tunnel was a pressure seal of Farworlder technology, a sort of membrane that allowed water through but held the crushing pressures of the deep sea at bay.

The six of them huddled together at the center of the tube. Nia held Garun's left shoulder; Cephan held his right. The princeling's shell was nestled in Garun's lap. Ar'an wrapped its tentacles around Dyonis's side to bind his wound closed. Dyonis began the drone that focused energy. Since he was only one, as opposed to the ten of the Low Council, Dyonis had to choose carefully where to focus his magic. Nia noticed he focused on the Farworlder prince.

Garun shuddered under her arm, and Nia held him closer to warm him. Little tentacles began to rise, wavering, out of the nautilus shell. The long tentacle with the circle of talons on the tip rose up, higher and higher.

"Do you have the name ready, Garun?"

"Yes," Garun growled through gritted teeth.

"All right. I'm going to help you." Nia grasped Garun's right hand, and she lifted it into position to receive the slap from the Farworlder tentacle.

Suddenly, she saw the knife in Cephan's hand. Too fast for her to intercept it, the knife plunged into Garun's chest.

"*Cephan!* What—"

Cephan reached across with his other hand to grab the prince's tentacle, and stopped it from touching Garun's hand. Garun cried out in pain and arched his back, spilling the Farworlder shell off his lap. Ar'an scooped up the shell in its membranes and swam to the far end of the tunnel.

Nia jumped up and pushed Cephan off of Garun. "What are you doing? What are you doing?" she screamed at him.

"I was going to be Avatar!" he yelled back. "I was going to be the greatest Avatar there had ever been! Look!" He pushed the hair back from his forehead, revealing the long scar. "Ma'el is a physician. He put an oculus into my head. I already have some Farworlder powers. I was able to use them—I touched your mind, and you felt it."

"That was *you*," Nia whispered in wonder. Her heart hurt within her chest. So many shocks, but this was the worst of all.

"Ma'el thought he was going to take over Atlantis. But I was going to use my power to control him. I just wanted to help my people, Nia. It was our turn, our time!" He stopped, his voice quieter but still urgent. "I still love you, Nia. We could be the most powerful pair in Atlantis. We could found a new clan! Just let me receive the mark!"

Nia looked over her shoulder at Ar'an, crouched defensively beside the pressure seal. "I don't think Ar'an's going to give you that chance." She knew the strength of an adult Farworlder. Even Cephan would not be able to break that grip. "Dyonis, can you heal Garun?"

Dyonis was hunched over Garun, trying to press his wound shut. But the water around them was rapidly turning red with Garun's blood. "I can't save him, Nia. The prophecy is fulfilled after all."

"Look," Cephan cried, "the little squid is going to die if it doesn't get to join with someone. Give it to me! I'm ready! I'm healthy. I can take it! Then I'll help you defeat Ma'el."

"Why is it," asked Dyonis, "that somehow I don't trust you? You speak of love, and yet you have murdered Nia's blood kin before her eyes."

Cephan's face contorted into a mask of rage. "As if I should trust you, who used your great powers to cheat in the Trials!" Brandishing the knife, he rushed at Dyonis. "Tell your creature to release the prince, or I will kill you!"

"I will tell Ar'an no such thing," said Dyonis. "And I am already dying, so your threat means little to me. And if you try to harm Ar'an, he will kill the little prince himself."

Cephan raised the knife. "We will see."

"No!" Nia cried. Grabbing Cephan's arm, she pulled him aside. Desperate, she snatched the Sword of Peace from the scabbard at Dyonis's side and swept it up to point at Cephan. "I won't let you harm another member of my family!"

Cephan narrowed his eyes at her. "I will do what I must, Nia. Drop the sword, and I will give you another chance."

"Chance at what?" cried Nia. "To be with a murderer? No!" An image came clearly to her mind then. An image sent by Ar'an and Dyonis. *The valve over your head, Nia. Open it. Quickly.*

Nia kicked off and shot up to the steam pipe overhead. Tucking the sword under one arm, she reached up and turned the valve wheel.

"What are you doing?" Cephan cried. "You'll kill us all!"

"We shall see," Nia said.

With a mighty *whoosh* and a groan, the pipe separated, and a blast of hot water struck Nia in the chest. The seal to the tunnel, made to withstand pressure from the outside but not from the inside, blew open. Nia tumbled out of the tunnel alongside Ar'an, and rose up along the Dome of Atlantis. The pressure was crushing, pressing her gills tightly shut so she could not breathe. She caught one last glance of the city, beautiful and dead before her. *So this is how it ends*, she thought, as her mind emptied to blackness.

Chapter Sixteen

Nia's back was hot. Aching. Something was pressing her hard against the floor. She felt heavy, oh so heavy, as if all her body was made of wet sand. *I'm in a dry room*, she thought. *What am I doing there?* For a moment she tried to open her eyes, but it was too bright, too bright. She kept them firmly shut.

Then the coughing began. First a little. Then a great heaving as she gasped and gulped air in and vomited water out of her lungs and stomach. Again and again she coughed and coughed. *I am dying*, she thought. And then, *But aren't I already dead?*

She raised herself up on her elbows and heaved the last of the seawater from her lungs. Her hands and arms were sinking into a soft, gritty surface. She stayed in that position, thinking only about breathing, breathing. *Breathing air?*

Nia tried to open her eyes again. Slowly, one eye. Too bright. Slowly, the other eye. Too bright. Slowly both eyes.

Blinking constantly, she could not make sense yet of what was around her.

She was lying on sand, wet sand. She could hear a roar and hiss behind her that bore no relation to any sound she knew. She tried to jump up, which in water would have been simple. Instead she merely sank back onto her knees.

Nia had to squeeze her eyes shut before she could look again. There were black-and-gray rocks ahead of her, rising to hillocks with green stuff on them, like moss but not wet. And beyond that, tall green-and-brown branchy things . . . trees! Nia suddenly remembered the term from the Academy, and wall paintings she had seen. *I'm on a shore. I'm on a beach. I'm on LAND!*

Panicked, Nia tried to turn around, but something was caught on her leg. She looked—it was Ar'an. Now flattened, stretched out, dried and stinking, its huge eyes milky in death. *Ar'an saved my life*, she thought. And then another thought came, one she didn't want to face. But she knew it was true; if Ar'an was dead, then so was his Avatar.

Nia carefully moved her leg out from under Ar'an's stiff tentacles, forcing herself to concentrate on the present. Slowly, legs spread apart, she was able to raise herself up, wavering, wavering. Her blue-and-silver gown stuck to her skin. Some of the silver scales had fallen off. Nia plucked at the material, trying to get it to hang right. Then she looked up and saw . . . the sea.

It stretched away from her as far as the horizon. Sunlight danced on its surface; its swells waved and beckoned to her. Nia had never seen anything so beautiful in her life. She stepped toward it, nearly falling over with each step. She stopped as the surging seafoam swept over her feet.

What if Ma'el and Cephan are waiting for me out there? I am so weak, I couldn't fight them. I don't know where I am. What if Atlantis is very, very far away? We were always taught that a mermyd alone, Outside, in the open sea, does not have much chance of a long life. There is so much danger. What am I going to do?

Nia felt an itching on her right palm. She rubbed her hand on her thigh, but it wouldn't go away. She raised up her hand and looked at it.

There was a sun-shaped scar on the palm. The prince's mark.

Nia staggered back. *How? How did I get this?* Ar'an had been holding the Farworlder prince. *And Ar'an was holding me. Is it possible as I slept . . . it must be so! The prophecy has been entirely fulfilled! I am the Avatar.*

A vision suddenly smote her mind. A box of wood,

open to the sky. A young land-dweller's face, full of curiosity. A black, shiny creature with a long beak and skinny legs—a bird! A low dwelling made of stone. A scowling face with a gray beard and wrinkled skin. *Stop!* Nia sank to her knees in the sand.

The Farworlder prince is alive. Nia knew this; it sang in her blood. But for how long? *We have not done the changing of the blood, the Naming. If I do not find the prince, it will die. I will die. Within seven days, the stories say.* The prince was no longer on the beach. And he was very afraid. Nia was going to have to search to find him.

Somehow, Nia found the strength to stand again. She glanced up the shore. There was something lying some yards away. Nia headed toward it. It took her some practice to adjust her footing to the slick stones, and then to the soft sand that ground against her feet. Several times she nearly fell over. *How do land-dwellers manage?* she wondered. *I suppose they are used to it.*

She saw strange, parallel ruts in the sand that seemed to stop at one point along the beach. At last, Nia approached the object lying on the sand. Her heart caught in her chest as she recognized who it was. She fell to her knees beside the body of Dyonis. Nia ran her hands over his gills, his chest, even though she already knew what she would find—no breath, and no pulse in his neck. He was dead.

"No. No, no." Even after seeing Ar'an, she had held on to a slim hope for Dyonis, and now it was gone. Nia felt water come to her eyes and overflow down her cheeks. Her breath became ragged and gasping. She lay her head on Dyonis's shoulder and cried for a long time.

At last she raised her head, unable to sob anymore. "You were right, Father," she said. "You and the High Council. Your prophecy was correct. I did become the Avatar. I did help bring disaster, by trusting Cephan and letting Ma'el into the Great Hall. And now I have to make it right. If it takes the last breath in my body, I must atone for what I have done, and save the prince and Atlantis."

The sun was sinking toward the horizon. *What happens when it enters the sea?* she wondered. And then she remembered her Academy teachings that the sun, in fact, at no time touches Earth.

She gazed at Dyonis's body and wondered what to do with him. *Should I leave him as he is?* Undersea, in Atlantis, the dead might be towed away by dolphins to drift with the tide, and to feed other denizens of the ocean. Sometimes a mermyd would stipulate that he or she become feed in a hatchery, or mulch in a kelp farm. None of that was possible here.

Land-dwellers, Nia had heard, buried their dead in the ground. She knew she did not have the strength or time to make a hole big enough. Some land-dwellers burned their dead, but Nia had no idea how to make fire.

She stood and grasped Dyonis's tail fin and tried to drag him back into the water. But he was too heavy, and she was too weak. *Besides*, she thought, noting the movement of objects in the surf, *the water would just bring him back in to shore*.

At last, she found a pile of beached seaweed and contented herself with covering Ar'an and Dyonis with that. Strange, tiny creatures, like krill, hovered and buzzed around her arms and hands as she spread the seaweed over.

Then Nia said words of farewell to them both. She went back to the strange ruts in the sand. *I have the feeling these lead somewhere. As I have no other thoughts of where to go, I will follow them. Guide me, my prince. Help me find you, before we both lose our lives.*

With one last long, lingering gaze at the sea, Nia turned to begin a journey into a new and completely unfamiliar world.